# UNTO THE THIRD GENERATION

## A Novella of the Future

By

**Rosemary and Larry Mild**

Magic Island Literary Works  •  Honolulu, HI  •  2017

**Interior book design by Larry Mild.**
**Cover design by Marilyn Drea, Mac-In-Town, Annapolis, MD.**

Library of Congress Cataloging-in-Publication Data
Mild, Rosemary P. ; Mild, Larry M.
Unto the Third Generation
Mild, Rosemary P. ; Mild, Larry M.
ISBN 978-0-9905472-2-8

First Edition 2017

**10 9 8 7 6 5 4 3 2 1**

# Dedication

For our beloved grandchildren—
Alena, Craig, Ben, Leah and Emily

For our wonderful children—
Jackie and Myrna

For our marriage—soul mates, partners, lovers

# Acknowledgments

We could fill an entire volume with the names of all the family members, dear friends and acquaintances who are loyal fans of our books.  You are all precious to us and give us the ultimate push to continue our writing. We owe special thanks to the following for their expertise, advice, feedback and encouragement:

• Diane Farkas, our eagle-eyed proofreader and dear friend.

• Sisters in Crime/Hawaii Chapter.

• Hawaii Fiction Writers.

• Mystery Writers of America.

# Disclaimer

***Unto the Third Generation*** is entirely a work of fiction. The plot and the events therein are of the authors' imagination and invention. All characters are fictitious and any resemblance to persons living or dead is purely coincidental.

# Contents

# Other Books by the Milds

- *Locks and Cream Cheese*
- *Hot Grudge Sunday*
- *Boston Scream Pie*
- *Death Goes Postal*
- *Death Takes A Mistress*
- *Death Steals A Holy Book*
- *Cry Ohana*
- *Murder, Fantasy, and Weird Tales*
- *The Misadventures of Slim O. Wittz*

# Other Books by Rosemary

- *Miriam's World—and Mine*
- *Love! Laugh! Panic!*
  *— Life with My Mother*

Chapter 1

# The Remarkable Year

THE PRIME NUMBER YEAR 2039 WOULD HAVE BEEN unremarkable except for two significant events. The first event marked a giant breakthrough for the well-being of all mankind. The second posed a potential threat to the continued existence of all mankind. It would be the beginning of the third generation before the impact of these two events clashed.

* * * *

Today nearly a thousand dignitaries from all over the world have come to Italy to celebrate their joint achievement: the development of a new synthetic food process. The scientist most responsible for this world-shaking event is Umberto Valeriani, a native Neapolitan. He coordinated the process several years earlier in Palermo, Italy. Just a week ago today, Synthomanna was approved for worldwide distribution.

At the head table in the vast convention hall in central Rome, Umberto stood and grandly raised his wine glass. "I drink to the end of hunger on this planet. *Salute!*" Glasses clinked like chimes. A wave of toasts in many languages reverberated throughout the assemblage.

Umberto, a short, stocky man with a trim brown beard, had successfully combined the efforts of three brilliant scientists. He set his glass down and continued. "The esteemed colleague on my right, Edvard X. Holgren, has applied a series of new catalysts and processing techniques to certain fibrous pellets that can imitate the consistency and appearance of almost any food currently known to man. Think of it: the crispness of a cracker, the soft texture of a pudding, the tender chew of a filet mignon, or the melt-in-your-mouth mashed potato. Thanks to him, these fiber pellets are easily and economically processed from a singular variety of tubers now growing all over the world. These particular tubers require little water and minimal chemical additives, and the resulting pellet is extremely lightweight to ship. Edvard has been working on this idea for twelve years. This great humanitarian has spent a good deal of his personal time and money trying to get his so-called 'dry manna' tubers to grow nearly everywhere. I give you Edvard X. Holgren of Stockholm, Sweden."

Edvard pushed his chair back and stood as the sound of applause rose to an uncanny roar. "Thank you, thank you. Being able to mimic a desired consistency and appearance represents only a portion of the collective achievement honored here today. After all, what is food without flavor? My good friend Vassally Krackob, hearing of my work, was eager to join forces with me. He had developed nineteen basic condiments which, if used in the correct combinations and amounts, could just about duplicate the flavor of any foodstuff in the world larder. His condiments are processed easily and economically from plentiful mineral and plant sources.

"The key to Dr. Krackob's success is an agent used to lock in the desired flavor. It prevents anyone from flavor-tampering afterwards. This is not the first time that he has achieved world prominence. In 2024 he developed a harmless flavor only a desperately hungry person would and could eat. That locked-in flavoring additive was used to keep hunger relief supplies from finding their way into the black markets of the Third World nations. The locking agent ensured that the supplies were of value only to the starving and not to local opportunists. I introduce Vassally Krackob of Moscow, Russia."

# Unto the Third Generation

Dr. Vassally took the microphone. "Thank you very much. But what of food value? Shouldn't the meals we eat contain the elements our bodies need and crave? Dr. Sarah Bet Moshez has found an inexpensive way to add nutrients and pleasing taste to edibles lacking either one. Her process simulates a real meal. She is an Israeli scientist, a nutritionist working with the undernourished in a nearby Arab community. My colleague Umberto sought her out. Sarah was so enthusiastic about his project, nearly paralleling her own, that she immediately joined in. Working closely with Umberto, those two found a way to infuse essential vitamins and nutrients into the flavorful, substantial, and satisfying synthetic food forms developed by the rest of us. The trick here was to infuse without disturbing the molecular structure or flavor. I give you the lady who accomplished that goal in five short months, Dr. Sarah Bet Moshez."

This time the applause and glass-clinking included a few brazen wolf whistles at the dark-skinned, dark-haired beauty who now stood before them at the head table. "We thank you. The four of us collaborated on creating the first ideal synthetic food. We call it Synthomanna, our trademark legally registered with the European Union. Of course, Synthomanna must be marketed as synthetic. For the first time in history, with special additives, man can effectively control weight, calories, flavor, consistency and bulk."

In a sobered voice, Sarah continued. "To be sure, there will be a great economic impact on the current food industry. Much land use and industrial muscle will be directed elsewhere, as needed. There will be some fortunes lost and some gained. The same is true with jobs. As always, the skeptics will have to be won over and the diehards will fall by the wayside. We predict that within five years Synthomanna will be on everyone's table. But most important, it will be available in famine-ravaged countries. We expect much anger and protesting, but this time the world's malnourished and starving will come first." Sarah raised her wine glass and shouted in Hebrew, "*L'chaim*, To life."

A young American scientist deep in the audience sprang

out of his seat and asked, "With all due respect, aren't you rushing things a bit?" He gazed slowly around the great hall, his eyes deliberately locking on those of many individuals. "My distinguished colleagues, we haven't heard a word on the results of human trials. Have there been any? That is, any on the long-term effects of synthetic foods? Your revolutionary process goes well beyond genetically modified foods."

It would be years before the answers to those questions were learned.

* * * *

The second significant event of 2039 was the outbreak of a previously unknown and deadly disease. The earliest cases appeared in Florence, Italy (*Firenze* to the locals). When one physician there compared the fiery fevers to those of influenza, another physician ironically called it Infirenza. The name stuck and was thereafter used worldwide. But it was not like any strain of flu known previously. Already, Infirenza was spreading slowly across Europe in small geographic gulps with no identifiable carrier agents.

In the United States, Government officials noted this threat to an entire continent and designated a federal health agency to head off a potential epidemic. The Institute for Prevention and Control of Infectious Diseases in Chicago, Illinois, began tracking Infirenza and trying to learn more about it. Calvin Meechum, MD, was put in charge and given an office and adjoining conference room on the fourth floor of the East Building. Calvin answered to the chief of the Institute. There was no way to know when—or even if—Infirenza would hit the United States, but they wanted to be prepared. Scientists assumed that, sooner or later, the virus would invade the U.S. via American travelers returning home from Europe and/or Europeans already infected who were vacationing or on business in the U.S.

Taking his seat at the head of the conference table, Calvin greeted his team of distinguished physicians and Ph.D. scientists. Although a slight man with rounded shoulders and seemingly mild manner, his keen gray eyes and no-nonsense approach commanded respect. "I'm new at this Infirenza thing, so how about you bring me up to date," said Calvin. "Sharon, what are the symptoms?"

Dr. Sharon O'Rourke looked older than her thirty-eight years. Researching the epidemic had already threaded her auburn hair with thick streaks of gray. She pulled a file from her briefcase and passed it to Calvin. "Essentially," she said, "the primary symptoms of this emerging disease are the fevers progressing from very low level to extremely high over time."

"How high and how much time?" asked Calvin.

"Quite high—enough to cause death. Secondary symptoms caused by the Infirenza fever are agonizing headaches, as well as significant body fatigue and loss of sleep. The time span of the disease? A matter of months or sooner, depending on the initial health of the patient."

"No survivors?"

"None that we've heard of."

"How is Infirenza diagnosed?" asked Calvin. "How would it differ from, say, the flu before it's too late to treat?"

Sharon shook her head. "That's just it. The early stages are no different. There's almost no way to tell before it's too late."

Dr. Meecham wrote a few notes on a lined pad. When he raised his head he asked, "Then at what point is the diagnosis confirmed?"

Sharon slid a second page across the table to him. "We've collected some data on this—not nearly enough, but the best available so far. The one linking factor is that the fevers are cyclical in nature. Initial cycles are less intense, even moderate in some cases, leading doctors to think they're dealing with simple flu. Then the fevers attack in ever-increasing torrents, often deceptively lapsing into shrinking, cooler periods that vary for each patient. Painful deaths occur when the fevers peak beyond human tolerance. Most patients have died in the first few months. Others died shortly after. But many live normal, otherwise healthy, lives during the cool phase. They appear to be cured. Unfortunately, this phase never lasts. From the data we've been able to obtain, no one has ever escaped Infirenza's grip."

"What kind of periods are we talking about here?" Calvin's fingers fidgeted with his pen.

"Onset cycles vary with fever periods lasting from four to six days, followed by no-fever relief periods without symptoms, also lasting four to six days. The fevers increase in intensity in succeeding cycles for months until the unbearable terminal cycle. The intensities in that terminal cycle can't be measured beyond the 106 degrees maximum when death occurs. Terminal cycle periods vary from two to four days."

Calvin challenged her. "You used the words 'almost no way to diagnose early.' What did you mean by almost?"

"It has to do with treatment. None of the fever-reducing techniques or drugs seem to mitigate a patient's fever," replied Sharon.

"So we're stuck with an emerging fatal disease that we can't treat and are having trouble diagnosing," Calvin said flatly. "Have we found a cause for this fever?"

"It has to be infectious somehow," admitted Sharon. "But even with all the brain scans and autopsies, we're still in the dark. There's no sign of accompanying unidentified viral or bacterial activity. We're still looking."

"Our team has performed all kinds of tests—without success," Dr. Samuel Unser broke in. "We tried injecting contaminated body fluids into laboratory mice without luck. Exchanging ambient air between patient and mice disproved any of the suspect airborne paths." Dr. Unser hesitated before delivering another perplexing report. "Only three human trials have been performed. Three Italian prisoners, seeking relief from their life sentences, offered to be guinea pigs, if you'll excuse the expression, in clinical trials. They risked their lives to be exposed in similar tests. Oddly enough, none contracted the disease, and all three were rewarded with some finitely lower prison term."

Calvin scowled. "Nothing helpful there." He turned to the final member of his team, Harvey Adams, the scientist tracking the origin of the disease. "Harvey, have we identified patient zero yet and his or her location?"

"Yes, sir! Vitorio Deluca. He died twenty-two months ago in Florence, Italy. That's how Infirenza got its name. You know, the Florence-*Firenze* thing."

"Yes," retorted Calvin, frowning in impatience. "I understand that. Does the disease have any particular path of least resistance or a favorable path? Does it seek anything tangible?"

"No, sir," Sharon replied. "The path is one of its own convenience. It creeps ever so slowly—one or two square kilometers per month, completely devastating everyone in its path."

Calvin momentarily stared into space while he tried to think of anything worthy to add. He laid down his pen, his expression grim. "That's it. Stay with it and keep me informed."

As they all filed out, one thought plagued each of them: Are we facing a pandemic? A worldwide disease?

Chapter 2

## Leonard and Francine

A GENERATION LATER, A BLACK CLOUD HUNG
over planet Earth. No one had ever been cured of the deadly disease. In November of 2059 nearly half the world's population had
died of Infirenza. Now the realization loomed: the end of mankind was marching closer. Infirenza had just leaped the Atlantic
and dug into Middle America with its mighty tentacles. Neither the
medical profession nor the scientific community had a solution.
Even Synthomanna, the perfect source of nutrition, couldn't help
stop the pandemic. Humankind could now feed the needy multi-
tudes, but couldn't save them from the inevitable.

* * * *

Neither Leonard Tall-Chief nor Francine Mapleton knew
anyone who had ever contracted Infirenza. Sure, they'd heard of
it, but they chose to dwell in that convenient zone of blind com-
placency. In fact, the two were totally unaware of each other's existence. Curiously, though, they had a number of traits in common.
They were both single, in their early twenties, and healthy-looking.
But more important, each had unknowingly contracted the deadly
disease sometime in the previous two weeks.

Leonard, of Cayuga Indian extraction, resided in Columbus, Ohio. The bruising six-foot-four, 240-pound Leo, as he preferred to be called, cut, welded and riveted iron and steel high

8

above the city's roofs. He loved his job and was an expert at it; he'd been doing it since he graduated from high school five years ago. When the first headache and sweats struck him early on Monday morning, Leo thought he had a hangover. Getting dressed became an extreme effort. The big guy felt as though he was dragging another man's body along with his own. He went to work anyway, navigating narrow beams at his high-steel construction site in midtown Columbus. Under the blazing morning sun, he narrowly escaped a fatal slip on the sixth level. A half-hour later he dropped a hammer into space. The foreman witnessed both incidents.

"Hey, Leo," he yelled. "You're sick. You look like death warmed over. Go on home, buddy."

"Aw, gimme a couple minutes." Leo ran a hand through his longish jet-black hair, clinging with sweat to his neck. "I'll be fine. I'll take two aspirin and be as good as new."

"No you won't," the foreman said. "Git the hell out of here before you kill yourself and somebody else, too."

Leo reluctantly rode the elevator bucket down to the ground and drove home, begrudging the day's loss of pay. The headaches got worse, accompanied by a high fever, forcing him to stay home on Tuesday, Wednesday and Thursday, nursing the four-day painful ordeal without much sleep. He was incapable of any sort of work until Friday, when he awoke in his recliner, refreshed and free of all symptoms. He had finally fallen asleep there the previous afternoon. He took a shower, dressed and headed for the construction site, where he put in two ten-hour days. He partied with the gang on Saturday night and watched NFL football all day Sunday. Monday and Tuesday were uneventful work days. But Wednesday morning he awoke once more with a fever and violent headache. He was able to get a doctor's appointment for that same afternoon.

Forty-five minutes beyond the appointed time, a middle-aged nurse extracted him from the waiting room and recorded his blood pressure and temperature. Though she said nothing, Leo noted a look of concern on her kindly face.

A specialist in infectious diseases, Dr. E.W. Weng was in his mid-forties, but the deep lines furrowing his brow made him look as if his profession were taking its toll. Behind wireless glasses, he only emitted noncommittal grunts while conducting his examination. Leo sat up on the examining table, legs dangling over the side. Dr. Weng slid the cold stethoscope disk across the patient's smooth chest, then slapped it on his back.

"Take a deep breath," he prompted.

"Okay, but what the hell's wrong with me?"

The doctor ignored Leo's question and instead asked, "How long have you experienced this over-the-top fever and headache?"

"Just this morning, Doc, all morning and without a break."

"Any symptoms before today?"

"Uh…" Leo hesitated. He feared losing his job, but knew he had to tell the truth. "Last week, Monday through Thursday, I missed work. Popped aspirin and sleeping pills like candy." He shuddered with a sudden chill and wrinkled his face with intense pain.

Dr. Weng shook his head. "That could be dangerous. On a scale of one to ten, how severe were your symptoms at their worst?"

"Real bad, Doc. A ten," Leo admitted. "I had trouble sleeping and I couldn't read or even watch TV. All I could do was keep toweling myself off and drinking cold water. I didn't want to go through that again, so I made this appointment."

"Which symptoms are worse—that is, more intense? Today's? Last week's? Or no difference?"

"Today! No question about it. The top of my head wants to explode right now. I don't know how much more I can take." Leo ran a handkerchief from his pocket over his dripping face. He waited while the expressionless doctor wrote a half-page into his medical history.

"Doc, what gives? What's wrong with me? Is it…?"

"I'm afraid so, Leo. I can't be completely sure for at least another distinct fever cycle, but it does look like you have Infirenza. I know what you're thinking, but let's not jump to conclusions until next week and hope that the definitive third fever cycle doesn't arrive."

"You're pretty sure already, aren't you? Isn't there any cure, Doc? Can't you give me any relief?"

Dr. Weng shook his head slowly. "Yes. I can write you a stronger prescription, but I'm told narcotics have little or no effect on this type of pain. The fact that the aspirin and sleeping medications you've been taking have proved ineffective is a distinguishing symptom of Infirenza."

"How long have I got to live, Doc?"

Dr. Weng pressed his thin lips together and paused. In his professional experience, this was the hardest question to deal with. "Ninety-five percent of these cases fall in the three-to-five month span."

"There isn't even a tiny bit of hope, then?" Leo wiped the icy beads of sweat on his forehead with an already sopping handkerchief.

"The journals tell me there's a whole lot of research going on," said Dr. Weng, "but no viable cure. Unfortunately, the only useful bit of information to come out of it so far is that Infirenza has not spread to the Arctic regions. Statistics from the IPCID have shown no cases occurring there." He pulled a few sheets of paper toweling from the dispenser and handed them to Leo.

"Huh? What's the IPCID?"

"Sorry," Dr. Weng said. "It's the Institute for Prevention and Control of Infectious Diseases, the top federal agency."

Leo's voice took on a desperate tone. "What if I moved to Eskimo country, Alaska or Iceland or someplace like that?" he asked, gratefully putting the paper towels to good use.

"I've heard that lower-temperature environments do inhibit extreme body temperatures in some small way. You might live a week or two longer," said Dr. Weng. "The cooling approach has been tried, but indicated no improvement in the quality of life.

The result is inevitably the same: premature death."

"Then what the hell good is all that damn Arctic information?" asked Leo.

Dr. Weng would have preferred taking Leo into his office, where they could sit in comfortable chairs for the subject he was about to broach. But he could see that his patient—straightforward and intelligent—was in no mood for delaying niceties. He proceeded. "Leo, have you ever heard of cryogenic preservation?"

"Is that where they put people to sleep in an icebox?"

"In a sense, yes. It's controlled freezing, a means of slowing down human body functions and organ activities to the point where life is virtually imperceptible. Scientists have been working on cryogenic preservation for many generations. But from what I've read in the journals, the first whole body to be preserved and revived after ninety-six hours didn't occur until 2043. That was sixteen years ago, and the volunteer subject experienced a significant side effect: considerable memory loss. I'm afraid further research in that area has been slowed because volunteers are unwilling to commit to longer durations."

"Does it actually work?" asked Leo. "I mean, does it cure Infirenza?"

"Absolutely not. The original concept was to induce a deep, deep sleep—a state of cryogenic life-suspension—for the human body to possibly endure light-years of intergalactic space travel and finish a normal life after returning to civilization and resuscitation."

"Holy crap!" Leo interrupted. "That sounds like astronaut stuff—*Planet Rangers*, maybe."

Dr. Weng smiled wryly. "Yes, it does have that ring to it. Those Arctic statistics opened a second possibility: to outlast life-threatening diseases until either a cure is found or the disease peters out. How long might that take? One can only guess."

"Is it safe? I mean, a guy could die in one of those contraptions."

Dr. Weng's hand went to his narrow chin. "Apparently, a

number already have. According to the *Heartland Medical Journal*, the recent short-term tests were 98 percent successful. However, no test has spanned more than five years. No one knows the effects on the body of a much longer term. Would life be the same afterward? Would life eventually seep away at some point beyond the five-year mark? Would body form, function and capacity erode to the point of disuse or rejection?"

"Hey, five years is better than five months and maybe they'll come up with a cure by then. What do you think, Doc?" Leo mopped his face one more time.

Dr. Weng shrugged his shoulders. "Anything's possible."

"Doc, how does a guy like me sign up for this icebox thing?"

"I'm not sure. There's a company called Hybernautics. The president, Dr. Horace Richards, is running the program out of his family trust. The selection criteria have been rather unclear—so much so that I wonder if there's a deliberate attempt to make their work secretive."

"Jeez, Doc, I bet everybody and his uncle is trying to sign up for a thing like this."

"You might be right about that, Leo. I could write you a letter of recommendation if you like, but with Infirenza already in your system, I doubt that you'd be a likely candidate."

Leo actually hopped off the examining table, his large body more erect than when he'd arrived. "I'd appreciate it if you'd recommend me, Doc, whatever my chances." He shivered as he pulled on his flannel shirt.

Dr. Weng nodded. "I should send you to the hospital, but they haven't had any available beds for nearly a month. Go home and get as much bed rest as you can. Call me if anything changes." After ushering Leo out, he walked in frustrated silence back to his office, an emotional twinge striking his heart.

* * * *

**F**rancine Mapleton, better known as Fanny, lived in a suburb of St. Louis, Missouri. Five-foot-three and sturdily built, she waited tables in a popular diner six days a week. Regular male customers searched out her booths to be seated. They found her manner perky and her looks fetching, especially the frizzled, unruly blonde hair that circled her round face, accentuating dimples on both cheeks.

Fanny attributed her aching limbs to her nine-hour shift at Mickey's Diner. She kept looking at her watch: 10:15. Forty-five minutes to closing time. It was only twenty minutes since she last looked. Long shifts were not unusual for her, but her body's all-over ache certainly was. She ran the back of her hand across her forehead and pushed a hank of damp curls off her flushed face.

The customers in booth six had just gotten up, leaving a five-dollar tip before pushing out the door. Fanny tucked it into her apron pocket, then took an empty tray and started over to the booth, seriously wondering if her legs would drag the rest of her body that far. She set the tray on the left-side booth bench and sluggishly piled it up with the empty dishes, coffee cups, silverware, and balled-up paper napkins. Dimly, she knew she should let the busboy do it, but she wasn't thinking clearly. Leaning over the table, she began swishing a wet rag in a wide arc to clean it, but every inch of her body seemed to resist, pulling her away, as though she were in a slow-motion movie scene. She tried to steady herself by gripping the edge of the table with her left hand, but her palm felt sweaty, and slid away. Still clutching the rag, she felt herself falling backward. The room flashed and swirled before her eyes. The ceiling tiles were the last thing she saw before darkness enveloped her.

Ten minutes later, she regained consciousness and flailed about, trying to avoid a repulsive odor, what she thought was a spray cleaner, but when her eyes focused, she saw that it was an ammonia ampoule following her jerky evasive tactics. Two men in gray uniforms knelt next to her. Fanny could hear Mickey's voice in the background barking orders. A blood pressure cuff on her arm hurt at first, and then let out a final whoosh of air. Her head throbbed. She uttered a long, agonized moan.

One of the kneeling men leaned in to speak. "How are you feeling, ma'am?"

"Terrible, I've never felt so bad in my whole life," she said. "But who are you, and why am I on the floor?"

"Emergency Medical Services, ma'am. Your boss called 911. We're EMTs. We found you this way. Apparently, you fainted and fell next to this booth. As near as I can determine, you have no broken bones, although you may have experienced some bruising from the fall. Can you tell me if anything else is wrong?"

"Oh, my head," she wailed. "I've got the worst splitting headache. I never get headaches. Can't you give me something for it?"

"I can't. You may have a concussion." He swung a penlight back and forth in front of her eyes. Her eyes followed for a few seconds and then broke away.

"And I'm so...so hot, I'm melting," she told him, her voice quivering. "Mickey, Mickey," she yelled into space. "Isn't the air on? Isn't that lousy air conditioner working?" She tried to roll over on one side to sit up, but the gentle hand of the EMT restrained her. "You're not going anywhere, young lady. You've got a fever of 104. Lie back. We're transporting you to a hospital."

* * * *

**T**hree unnerving hospital days took their toll on Fanny Mapleton, At some point during the diagnostic questioning, she admitted to having flu symptoms nearly two weeks earlier. Even though the doctors were already thinking Infirenza, and told her so, the symptoms suddenly disappeared and she was released. At home with her mother, she began to feel like her old self. But she anxiously awaited the frightening prospect of the third cycle of symptoms.

Fanny convinced Mickey that she wasn't contagious and returned to work a week later. After all, no one knew how the disease was transmitted. Body fluids, direct contact and airborne emissions had all been eliminated through the Institute's exhaustive testing in Chicago. Her diner co-workers, including her best

friend, Edith, were not convinced; they treated her as a sort of
Typhoid Mary. The diner's patrons were uninformed, so they were
oblivious. Mickey was glad his restaurant had returned to its normal chaos.

It was a bustling breakfast shift on Fanny's second day
back, and the normally efficient waitress had turned into a spasm
of nerves. She precariously balanced a large round tray high on
her left palm and started for booth nine. This tray transported five
mugs of coffee, three glasses of orange juice, two tomato juice, a
small pitcher of milk for cereal, and a bottle of ketchup for the
three egg orders presently on the grill. She couldn't see the floor to
her left, so she never anticipated tripping over a briefcase parked
in the aisle. The tray flew forward, hurling porcelain and glass pro-
jectiles ten feet down the aisle. Coffee and juice sprayed over customers in booths on both sides of the aisle. Fanny fell to her knees,
then flat out. Rolling onto her back, she struggled upright to a
sitting position, pulled her knees in close, and began to sob with
shame and embarrassment.

At first, attitudes melted into sympathy. The customer
apologized for his wayward briefcase. Mickey helped her to her
feet and into an empty booth. Sliding in next to her, he did what
he could to comfort her. A busboy hurried to clean up the mess
and brought damp towels to the unlucky customers who got splat-
tered. But in five minutes the patrons began clamoring for service.
Orders were piling up in the window to the kitchen.

Mickey faced her, now with a look of annoyance. "I know
I should send you home, Fanny, but we're far too busy. Maybe I
can get someone else for tomorrow."

"No, Mickey," Fanny begged. "Don't do that. I need this
job."

"And I've got a business to run."

"I'll be fine. I just tripped over that damn briefcase. I know
I'm a little shaky right now, distracted too, but I can do it. Please!"

"Tell you what, girl," he said, sliding out of the booth. "You
take orders and give them the checks. Me and Edith will deliver the

food. How's that?"

"Sure! You're a dear, Mickey." She squirmed out of the booth, and straightened her uniform's skirt.

Ten minutes later, the diner was back to normal, humming like a well-oiled machine. As the week went on, Fanny found herself less distracted. *Maybe there won't be another fever cycle. I'm not going to think about it, I'm not going to think about it,* she intoned as if to hypnotize herself.

Think about it or not, the headache and fever returned nine days later with renewed strength and in screaming proportions. Fanny could not return to Mickey's Diner. Not then, not ever.

Chapter 3

## Decisions

**B**Y JANUARY 2059, WORLD GOVERNMENTS, ALONG with most of the pertinent scientific and medical teams, were receptive to the cryogenic suspension idea. But either they lacked the technology altogether or were totally unprepared to handle more than several dozen candidates—*cryonauts*, as they were called. Only the Swiss and American laboratories had any realistic capability. The applications to become a cryonaut spelled out the risks in meticulous detail. Nevertheless, these cryogenic gurus were inundated with more than a million volunteers, making selection a formidable task.

A U.S. Congressional Bipartisan Steering Committee decided that only the healthiest males and females in their twenties need apply to take the rigorous physicals. This criterion still left hundreds of thousands of candidates to pick from, a monumental task, to say the least. The committee's second decision established that the ratio of female-to-male should be two-to-one in order to maximize successful procreation should that need arise. A third decision required that intellectuals and athletes constitute at least two-thirds of the final cryopreservation slots.

The actual selection task fell to Dr. Horace "Horry" R. Richards, chief executive officer of Hybernautics, the largest cryogenics laboratory in the United States and an eminent pioneer in human hibernation. There were other cryogenics labs, but none with the modern life-suspension equipment and experienced team that his facility had. His scientists had been in the field for three decades—since the days of preserving microorganisms, tissues and small mammals.

Horry Richards remained a wealthy man, even after using the greater portion of his inheritance to finance the Chicago laboratory he started thirty-eight years ago. The H.R. Richards Family Fund allowed the lab nonprofit status, which slowed the hemorrhaging of his personal monies to keep it running. Between donations and Federal Government grants, the lab prospered. These same grants financed the now-famous life-suspension experiments that were so successful. The actual cryocapsules and surrounding technology were his toys, his creations.

Horry was a natural to head up the program. In his lab's earlier experiments, a small number of volunteers in each test group had remained in the cryogenic state for two or three years and emerged physically intact. The last group of ten volunteers had lasted five years. That test ended in 2053. No other lab could boast that achievement. Now Horry was taking a spectacular, giant leap: forty volunteers would be placed in a cryogenic state for at least five years and possibly much longer.

The astonishing number of applicants for this bizarre adventure raised a critical question. What did the volunteers hope to gain from life-suspension? Two primary reasons were revealed in the applications. Some applicants had debilitating, or even incurable, illnesses (other than Infirenza). They hoped that when they emerged from the cryogenic state in five years, a cure for their disease would be available. But many others had an element of the daredevil in them; they enjoyed extreme sports like mountain climbing in the Himalayas and skydiving. They yearned to be pioneers in this opportunity for life-extending science experiments.

At age fifty-nine Horry was a vain stickler about keeping up his good looks and athletic prowess. Six-foot-three, lean and agile, he spent three evenings a week playing serious handball. He and his Hollywood-gorgeous wife, Ellen, lived in a lavish North Shore mansion overlooking Lake Michigan. But that was her choice; Horry spent most of his waking day immersed in lab technology. He made big money, and she spent it, and the two tolerated one another. They had no children and few relatives. Perhaps the fact that his wife's Wicked-Witch-of-the-West mother spent huge blocks of time at the mansion led to his entrenched preference for long hours at Hybernautics.

This evening Horry sat at his teak power desk—half desk, half conference table—and pondered the big question. There were forty working cryogenic cradles available now. He'd called them cradles because the residents would awaken to a new life, a rebirthing of sorts. The press had been quick to call them coffins or—by more imaginative reporters—deadly human missile silos, especially after two volunteers had perished in an early failed experiment in 2045. "A mere mechanical malfunction," Horry cynically had called it, for in all of his other life-suspension experiments, the volunteers had emerged alive.

New cradles were being manufactured as he sat there. Renovations and new construction for this launch had been underway for months. Horry was confident that a lot more people would choose to be suspended in the not-so-distant future. But if he wanted to claim the associated groundbreaking fame, his future cradles had to be allocated quickly and efficiently. He smiled broadly as he visualized the selection plan coming together and gelling in his mind.

Finally, this very morning, he was ready. He pressed a lever on his intercom. "You can send them in now," he told his secretary.

The office door opened, and his four senior staff scientists entered and took seats opposite him. Horry acknowledged each of them with a friendly nod.

"Team, I believe I now have a viable plan we can run with. However, I will need help from each of your departments. Jon, you're the psychologist here. I want you to take charge of screening recruits mentally and intellectually. Because of the sheer numbers applying, you'll reject at the slightest doubt. I want to see draft questionnaires and interview planning as soon as possible. Understood?"

"Sure, Chief," answered Dr. Jon Seward, the youngest in the group. "Should have 'em by next Friday. We can begin screening on your say-so."

"Good," said Horry as he turned to the next man. "Fred, as my chief physician, I want you to take charge of medical screening. Again, reject liberally at the slightest doubt. That is, with one exception, which I'll go into shortly. I'd like to see your intended screening tests in the next few days."

"Of course, my good friend," replied the short, balding Dr. Fred Obermeyer.

"Your turn, Marie," said Horry, turning to the middle-aged matron in schoolmarm garb. "You're my math whiz. I need statistics. Your task will be to organize and manage the flow of recruits to and from the screeners and, more important, collect and track their personal, medical, psychological, and statistical data. I want to learn all I can about these candidates and their chances for success. Of course, I have been given the ultimate responsibility for picking the final forty from the information you three furnish me. I do not treat that responsibility lightly."

"I will do my best, Horry. You can depend on me," said Dr. Marie Fontaine.

"And finally, Ernie," addressed Horry. "You are in charge of training and acclimating the selected personnel to their assigned units. You know the drill. You've done it before."

"Of course, Boss, I'm on it," said Dr. Ernest Baer, nodding with his full head of bushy salt-and-pepper hair and ballooning brows to match.

"And now to my plan," said Horry. "Our forty cradles can easily be divided among three groups, twelve slots each, with a remainder of four slots. The Congressional Steering Committee has laid out general guidelines and left the nitty-gritty to us, mandating, however, that we proceed only with the approval of the Hyber-nautics Board of Directors. I'm pleased to report that I have their approval. Here is my grand plan. Each group will comprise eight women and four men.

"Group I shall be selected for their superior intelligence as determined by IQ testing, two each in six specific essential fields. I believe those fields should include mathematics, physics, chemistry, philosophy, literature and other creative arts."

"But, Chief, how…?"

"What is it, Jon?"

"How can we apply IQ measurements to literature and other creative arts like painting, sculpture, textiles, architecture, etc.? We're talking a different part of the brain, the right side."

"I see what you're saying," replied Horry. "Perhaps we could beef up the spatial, associative and compatibility aspects of the testing."

"Chief," retorted Jon, "that would take considerable time and effort to verify new testing components."

"May I remind you that we don't have that kind of time," rebuked Horry. "You'll have to patch something together, your best shot at it, anyway. And I trust you'll have it for me next week sometime."

A subdued Jon muttered, "Yes, sir, my best shot."

"Aren't we neglecting music?" asked Marie, daring to interrupt. "There's hardly room for music with only two cradles reserved for literature and other arts. That future world will be mighty bleak without music. May I suggest we find room for two versatile musicians in the second grouping?"

Horry frowned. "Group II is composed strictly of athletes." He leaned back in his leather swivel chair and squinted in contemplation. "You've got a point there, Marie. I suppose we could get away with two fewer athletes. I approve of this change. Replace them with musicians and/or composers."

"What about engineers, then?" asked Ernie. "I anticipate this new world will have plenty of practical problems to solve—

electrical, mechanical, structural, and communications problems. Who better than engineers to take on that challenge? How about two more of those athlete spots?"

"Now wait just a minute," snapped Horry, half-rising from his chair.

"Before you challenge Ernie, my friend," said Fred softly, "consider that I will be examining every candidate for maximal health. Don't you think we'll have a number of athletes among that culling? I recommend that fewer slots be taken by solitary athletes and more by those with skills and knowledge to contribute to rebuilding society. For example, let's keep three top athletes to ensure that the necessary dominant genes are present. Those three should be from the top winners who competed in recent Olympic pentathlon/decathlon events. They're the ones with all-around athletic prowess."

"I hear you, Fred, and I'm sure you're right about this," replied Horry, his voice conciliatory. He realized he'd overreacted. "Thanks for the new perspective."

"Who's in the third group that's so damned sacred?" asked Jon.

"Group III, the final group of twelve, is sacred in a way," Horry said. "The Board of Directors has already stipulated that it be comprised entirely of wealthy contributors. Their donations paved the way for our facility, equipment, and the inaugural cryogenic-instillation process. But also, these donors could create the additional permanent financial trusts needed to defray the high cost of perpetual upkeep for the groups undergoing cryosuspension. After all, one can only guess how long these volunteers will remain suspended, and there are bills to be paid. The rich should be selected according to whomever offers the largest trusts."

"What about the final four you spoke about?" asked Marie. "How will we select them? On what basis?"

"Ah, I thought you'd never ask," said Horry. "These four applicants will be the medical exceptions in the assignments. Two members of the Board of Directors are research medical doctors, and they've insisted on using these cryopreservation slots for an outright experiment." Horry leaned forward, set his elbows on the desk, and locked his fingers. "Quite frankly, friends, their demand has shocked the hell out of me. These clowns are requiring that two of the cryonauts be a male and a female who have already contracted and reached stage three of Infirenza. These two are to otherwise meet our highest medical standards. The remaining two, again a male and a female, are to form the control group for the first two."

Four pairs of eyes widened, reflecting what sounded to them like an extreme lack of logic.

Horry knew exactly what his trusted scientists were thinking and responded, "I tried to reason with the directors. I recommended that we select the final control-group twosome from our intellectual pool. But those idiots insisted that all four of those in Group IV are to be selected randomly, by lottery, from our generally healthy pool.

"Wow, what a waste!" said Jon. "It would have made room for two more creative slots."

"I agree," said Ernie. "Boss, where are we on the launch of the next wave of cryonauts?"

Horry slammed his fist down on the desk. "For chrissake, Ernie, why are you asking that? You should be totally focused on our ambitious current project. The here and now. If you must know, Congress has said a future launch can't take place for another seven years. We also need to analyze the current launch data and devote our attention to monitoring the entire life-suspension phase. We've already learned a great deal and this will be our chance to improve, adjust and prepare as necessary."

"Does this mean we'll continue to collect and analyze recruiting data during the upcoming suspension phase?" asked Marie.

"Of course," said Horry. "We've grabbed a leadership role in this field, and I have no intention of letting another firm overtake us. Our reputation is at stake."

Horry's penetrating eyes fixed on each expert's before he spoke again. "To repeat: I want those recruitment letters out of here by tomorrow so we can start testing applicants in two weeks."

Chapter 4

## The Lottery

**T**WO WEEKS HAD PASSED SINCE THE DECISION-making session at Hybernautics, and now the recruitment letters began arriving at selected homes all over the country. The world-threatening disease Infirenza continued to rage on, so these letters predominantly rained down on specific individuals chosen to preserve and conserve the human race. Groups I and II targeted candidates in all major areas of intelligence and talent. Group III zeroed in on candidates dedicated to financially ensuring the duration of the program. Group IV candidates constituted the statistical universe or pool from which the lottery was to function, that is, the random selection of the four medical types.

The letters to the exclusive Group IV pool generated a fierce range of emotions, from exhilaration to apprehension, and even to mocking disdain. Even though these candidates had volunteered to be considered, the threat of premature death and the risk of an uncharted, dangerous future triggered frightened reactions, especially if an applicant was currently disease-free. Somehow, word had gotten out that long-term memory loss had become an unexpected problem in three of the ten original five-year cryonauts.

Applicants who now felt skittish breathed a small sigh of relief. The letters explained that reporting for testing was compulsory, but commitment to the program was not. Even recipients who had enthusiastically applied could now change their minds and refuse to participate.

One of the recruitment letters was dropped into the mailbox of Leonard Tall-Chief. It remained unread for several days while he rode out the fevers, headaches and terrors of Infirenza's third wave. Those were days when patients didn't care whether a future was in store for them or not. There was a second letter in his box as well. Leo figured it was a termination notice and check from his boss for having missed six days of work this time. He tore into that envelope first and confirmed his suspicions: he had been fired, but at least the final check was generous. He knew he couldn't work high steel any more. It was far too risky. *But how can I support myself in the future?* Then it hit him. *I don't have to. I have no real future. I only have five months to live at the outside.* He tried his best to avoid a hang-dog look, even though no one else was around to see it.

Leo picked up the second letter and found that it had no return address, only the Hybernautics name and logo. With his large callused hands trembling, he ripped it open and read to himself. The more he read, the more excited he got. The contents instructed him to report for "multiple suitability examinations" at a King Avenue address in Columbus. The letter explained that if he met all the necessary requirements, he could be randomly selected, by lottery, into the cryonaut training program. These words gave Leo a fragment of hope for the first time in weeks. *Maybe there's a way out of this terrible illness yet.* The appointment was for Wednesday at 10:30 a.m. Leo looked at his calendar. *Today's Monday. Only two days off. That's one appointment I'm not going to miss.*

His craggy, square-chinned face lit up. *The letter of recommendation from Dr. Weng! It might give me an advantage. What the hell did I do with it?* He sat down at his desk and started pulling out drawers, raking through stacks of bills and papers. Nothing there. Then he remembered—he'd pinned it on the bulletin board over the kitchen table. Sure enough, the letter was there. He read through it again. *Am I overthinking this?* The words "random" and "lottery" stuck in his mind. He'd never even won five bucks in the Ohio state lottery.

The two days of waiting at home seemed endless and counterproductive. He wanted to get on with his next life, however far off that might be. This thought left him contemplating: *How large a group would I be chosen from? What are my actual chances of being chosen? What if I'm not among the chosen? What if I'm left behind to die like the rest of the Infirenza victims?* He knew those prospects would drive him crazy, so he decided to think about what he would do differently in his next life. *I should have married Cherie Goodwin, but I let her get away.* He shook his head at the memory of having betrayed himself. *Maybe there will be someone like her in the next life. Maybe I'll try college. Girls like guys that are smart. I could get a sports scholarship.*

Leo arose early on Wednesday morning after only four hours of fitful sleep. He finished his morning shave, shower and breakfast, unaware that he'd accomplished them at breakneck speed. The kitchen clock appeared to stand still at 7:30. *Three more hours. I'll leave early. There's bound to be some no-shows.* The full-length mirror on his bedroom door assured him that the image wearing creased jeans and a brand-new teal-blue sport shirt met his highest standards.

A twenty-minute walk to the King Street address found him pushing through the glass door into a large lobby. The wall-mounted directory indicated that Hybernautics commanded the entire second floor. A large elevator let him out in front of a reception desk, where he showed his letter of notification.

"Am I in the right place?" he asked, towering over the low desk and the young woman who staffed it.

"Yes," she said, after a quick scan of the letterhead. She hastily deposited it in a file basket. "Name?" she asked without referring to the To-Be-Filed basket.

"Tall-Chief, Leonard Tall-Chief. Am I early?"

The receptionist nodded, scanned a computer screen list,

and entered a few key strokes, acknowledging his arrival. "Thank you. Take any seat inside, Mr. Tall-Chief. Your name will be called when it's your turn." She pointed to the double doors on his right.

Leo walked through to find himself in a severe, unwelcoming room: uncarpeted vinyl floor; glaring recessed lighting; bare walls painted a sharp white. At least fifty people sat in padded folding chairs. Everyone seemed to be talking at once, creating an undecipherable din. He found an empty seat near the rear and sat down between two women. The one on his right was arguing with the sharply dressed, greasy-looking man on the other side of her.

"Leave me alone, you harassing womanizer," she said. "I don't want anything to do with you, and keep your hands to yourself. Go away!"

"Hey, fella. Let the lady be," grumbled Leo, leaning across the rather attractive woman to face her annoyer. "Go find another seat someplace else."

"Butt out, buster," the greaser answered. "Ain't none o' your beeswax. This is between the lady and me. I ain't goin' nowhere."

Leo rose to his feet and took two steps that placed his hulking frame directly in front of the wise guy. He growled a single word, "Now!"

The greaser took a second look at the towering Leo and squirmed. He grudgingly stood up, bumped past the others in the row, and disappeared into the crowd at the back. Leo returned to his seat just as the public address system announced, "John Flint 1056 to Room D, please, Mary Mulhenry 2033 to Room B, please."

"Thank you for rescuing me," said the grateful young woman on his right. "He was absolutely repulsive."

"Glad to be of help," returned Leo. "With all these people here, it looks like I'm gonna be hanging around a couple hours more. I came too early, thinking maybe they would take me sooner. I guess I figured wrong. Have you been waiting long?"

"Oh, maybe fifteen minutes longer than you," she answered. "My appointment is for 9:15." She looked at her watch. "It's 8:45 now. I guess I was a little apprehensive—I came early, too." She giggled nervously.

Leo noticed and tried to put her at ease. "My name is Leo. That's short for Leonard, Leonard Tall-Chief." *There's something about this gal that attracts me, but for the life of me I can't put my finger on it.* He wanted to know more.

"I'm Fanny," she murmured, hoping he wasn't another predatory guy. Then she regarded him for the first time: rugged, deeply tanned, clean-shaven, and quite gentlemanly. She liked what she saw and warmed accordingly. "My real name is Francine Mapleton."

"Fanny, not Franny?" asked Leo.

"Yeah. I had trouble saying my Rs when I was little girl, and the name stuck."

He chuckled. "How long have you lived in Columbus, Fanny?"

"I don't live here; my mother does. I'm came here temporarily to be with her."

"Oh, is she sick?" he asked.

"No, she's the picture of health at seventy-one." Fanny hesitated and slowly said, "I'm the one who's sick."

The public-address system bellowed, announcing more names. Several chairs scraped the tile floor.

"Infirenza?" Leo plied after the interruption.

She nodded. "I just wanted to be with my mom while I went through the rigors of the third wave. She tells me I keep calling out her name at night and crying the whole time. She says I'm her baby all over again."

Leo nodded sympathetically. "I just finished my third wave and you better believe I'm not looking forward to the next one. The lottery's my only chance. I sure hope they're quick about the choosing."

"I know what you mean, Leo. I don't know what I'm going to do if they don't pick me."

"If you don't mind me being nosy, where did you live before you came here, Fanny?"

"A small town called Webster Groves just outside St. Louis. I'm a…I mean I was a waitress at Mickey's Diner there. What about you? What do you do?"

"I work in construction, mostly tall buildings. Welding, riveting, manipulating high-steel beams—like that."

"Oooh, that sounds fearfully exciting," she said. "But isn't it dangerous, too?"

"It can be if you get careless. But it comes naturally. It's in my Indian blood—Iroquois and Cayuga, actually. A lot of us from the tribes are into high-steel work. The union's full of us."

"Francine Mapleton 0198 to Room G, please," bellowed the P.A. system.

"That's me," said Fanny as she stood up. "Good luck, Leo. I hope you get selected."

He stood up politely, face to face with her, and noticed her crystal-green eyes, small upturned nose and curling smile, accented by deep dimples. She extended her hand. He shook it, but what he really wanted to do was to kiss it gallantly. In fact, he wanted to gather up this lovely creature in his arms and kiss her properly on the lips, but he knew better. *With my luck she'd prob'ly sock me in the kisser.* He half-chuckled. *That wouldn't be so bad either.* He followed her high-heeled strut to Room G, his eyes glomming onto the almost-plump form in a blue pants outfit until he couldn't see her anymore. Leo returned to his chair. It was then that he felt an even stronger sense of loss.

* * * *

**F**anny felt pleasant, almost optimistic for the first time in weeks as she hurried toward the innocuous beige door marked with a big black G. She turned the handle and swung the door open, expecting to find an interviewer inside. Instead, she found only a small steel table and armless secretarial chair. A computer monitor and keyboard sat atop the table. The monitor screen read:

"Please take your seat and answer every question as best and as fast as you can. Depress the HOME key when you are ready for the first and all succeeding questions. Please start now."

The initial twenty questions dealt with her vital statistics, checking the accuracy of data in her application and the speed with which she responded. The next 100 questions seemed at times difficult, often ridiculous and sometimes repetitive. They checked general knowledge; aptitude; vocabulary; proficiency by means of word and math puzzles; and psychological suitability. The true-false and multiple-choice testing allowed thirty seconds per question, so that anyone not finished at the second hour's end would automatically be rejected.

Fanny finished with six minutes to spare, exhausted and drained. The optimistic, pleasurable feeling she had going into the testing was replaced with a sadness, a feeling she hadn't done her very best. *Why should they take me, anyway? I only have a high school diploma.* But a new screen message jumped to her attention. "Francine, you passed. Report to the medical center on the third floor for a physical." Her heartbeat quickened with relief; she'd made it this far. *Then why do I feel so rotten?* Walking down the long hall, she kept glancing about for her new friend, but didn't see him anywhere. *Now I know why I feel this way. We didn't exchange phone numbers. I don't know how to get in touch with Leo and he doesn't know how to get in touch with me either.* Fanny took the elevator one floor up to the medical center and exited into another reception area, this one filled with easy chairs and sofas. A dozen men and women sat comfortably engaged in conversations, as if they were friends at a cocktail party. Just when Fanny felt again like an outsider, a tall, thin woman approached her and pointed to her name tag.

"I'm Ruby Taylor. I'm going to be your guide and escort you through all the medical testing. First, I need to see some identification."

Fanny pulled her wallet from her purse and flipped it open to her driver's license.

"Good! Now if you'll please hold out your left arm so I can mark it with your name and ID number. Don't worry, it'll come off with a little alcohol." Ruby waited for Fanny's nod and then wrote 'F. Mapleton 0198' along her arm in inch-high characters. "Now, if you'll follow me, we'll get started."

Fanny followed her into a massive space hosting a labyrinth of smaller rooms. In the first one she exchanged her clothes for a hospital-type cotton dressing gown open in the rear and a pair of paper sandals. Ruby escorted her from room to room for a full-body CAT scan and MRI, stress testing, mammogram, eye exam, audio testing, blood and urine workups, electrocardiograph and electroencephalograph. All of the automated testing was performed with the most technologically advanced equipment; such that all results were available within minutes of the actual test.

When Ruby Taylor finally escorted her charge, fully dressed in her street clothes, out to the reception area, she was smiling. After wishing Fanny good luck, she handed her an envelope. Fanny immediately tore it open. She had passed. Her name and number had been added to the lottery list. She'd made the first cut! The candidates for cryonaut training would be selected the following Friday. Two alternates would also undergo training. She crossed her fingers and wondered how Leo had done.

* * * *

Indeed, Leo had also passed. Despite the disease, his examiners recognized a magnificent specimen of health and personality. Still, he couldn't stop thinking about his new friend. *Did she pass? I sure hope so. Will she be selected? Will I? Will both of us beat the odds and be selected? But what if I don't get in, what's next for me?* He let his brain shut down from following the next gruesome train of thought: maybe nothing but certain death.

Chapter 5

## **Plebes and Pledges**

**L**EO RIPPED OPEN THE ENVELOPE AS IF IT MEANT sheer survival for a starved and deprived animal. He had a good feeling about this letter. The Hybernautics name and logo struck a more affable high this time, but it could just as easily be a rejection. His heart pounded in tympanic thumps as he read the two-paragraph form letter with the fancy letterhead. The first paragraph congratulated him on being randomly selected from over 3,000 afflicted applicants. The wording gushed over how proud he should feel to enter the second cryonaut training course in human history. The second paragraph provided instructions for him to report immediately to a Chicago facility for training and preparation. The underscored word reflected a strong assumption that all applicants had already put their affairs in order during the waiting period. The letter was signed by Dr. Horace R. Richards, CEO and Director of Cryogenic Operations.

Leo's mind began to spin. *Class? Training? Preparation? What's that all about? I thought suspended hibernation meant you lie down in one generation and wake up several generations later. I've been going to bed and sleeping like a baby all my life. Nobody had to teach me how to do that. Chicago on Monday? Whoa, gotta make arrangements. Let's see, nothing in the apartment worth anything. Got no family since Auntie Dee died. They'll repossess the car when I stop payments. Yeah, let the vultures pick over the rest.*

Leo re-read the letter. He was to bring only his identification and the clothes on his back. All his other needs would be provided by Hybernautics. *But wait! There's something else in the envelope.* The corners of an airline ticket, a boarding pass, and a pink Post-it protruded from it. He read closely all the details: a 9 a.m. Monday flight from Columbus to Chicago in seat 12B. A Hybernautics bus just north of the taxi stand would transport members of his training class to the company facility.

* * * *

**O**n Monday morning at 11 a.m. the silver and gray shuttle bus left Chicago's O'Hare airport bound for Hybernautics. All of Leo's "colleagues" appeared to be in their twenties and thirties; clean-cut but introspective, with absolutely no thoughts of co-mingling or camaraderie. They were valued human beings, acutely aware that they were leaving everyone and everything they knew to embark on a rare, risky journey—a journey into some ill-defined measure of time lying somewhere in the vague future. A more specific thought flashed through Leo's mind. *Fanny is not on the bus. She wasn't even selected. That's a bummer.* He simmered over that disappointment for many a mile.

An hour later, the bus turned into a remote wooded area and drove up to a wrought-iron, logo-emblazoned gate that interrupted a brick, high-walled complex. A surveillance camera atop one of two pillars supporting the gate scanned the length and breadth of the bus while the driver exchanged words with a voice over an intercom. Permission granted, the bus continued up a long, wooded drive lined with lush green hedgerows. It slowed around a small, well-manicured circle and stopped in front of a block-wide, three-story building. A reception committee of five awaited them as the sixteen candidates stepped off the bus. The committee escorted them inside the showroom; its walls were papered with larger-than-life photo montages of Hybernautics accomplishments.

After signing in, they were led into a first-floor theater with comfortably padded seats. There were more candidates than just those from his bus, but Fanny was not one of them. Again he felt ashamed. *Why am I having these thoughts? I'm going to sleep for a bunch of years. I'll worry about my love life when I get back.* He turned his attention to the front of the room. A tall man stood at the podium, commanding their attention with his black-framed glasses, a full head of wavy salt-and-pepper hair, and sharply trimmed goatee. Three men and a woman sat on the stage on either side of him.

"Ladies and gentlemen, I am Dr. Horace Richards, the president and chief operating officer of Hybernautics. Welcome to our facility. The rest of your group will arrive later this afternoon. Altogether there will be forty candidates and four alternates in your class. I admire and commend each of you for accepting our challenge to venture into the unknown. Your program for the next three weeks is neither rigorous nor painful. Before you are through you will learn everything there is to know about two critical—and, I might add, momentous—words: instillation and resuscitation. We expect your full attention to the instructions and details we will provide."

Lapsing into a sterner voice, he continued. "Of course, there are a few rules to be followed. One, because of contamination concerns, you will be restricted to designated free areas in the facility. You will abandon all current clothing and wear only approved garments. Everything you brought with you will be destroyed. Two, because of the possibility of interfering chemical reactions, you will adhere to the diet foods prepared for you. Three, because we are uncertain how to deal with pregnancy in cryogenic suspension, you will not engage with members of the opposite sex. Four, because we are dealing with fragile life, sensitive instrumentation and expensive machinery, we discourage all forms of rough-housing.

"From now until instillation you will enjoy our hospitality. Each accommodation comes with a queen bed, a recliner, a fully equipped writing desk, television and radio, and private bath/shower. The common area features a pool, Ping-Pong and gaming tables. Chess, checkers and board games are available to occupy your free time; however, there may be little of that."

Dr. Richards poured a glass of water and consumed most of it before he put the glass down. "In a few minutes you will be broken up into smaller groups and assigned a guide who will take you on a tour of the facility. At the end of the tour you will be given time to acclimate to your new quarters. By the way, your respective guides will be quartered nearby to assist you." His crow-black eyes scanned the group.

"Now I'd like to introduce the key members of my staff. On my far right is Dr. Jon Seward, Chief Psychologist. Next to him is Dr. Friedrich Obermeyer, Chief Physician. On my left is Dr. Marie Fontaine, Chief Statistician. And next to her on my far left is Dr. Ernest Baer, Training Chief. Their office doors, as well as my own, always remain open to you for advice and clarification. I wish you every success." He half-turned, paused, then returned to the podium in a calculated move to break the thick tension. "By the way," he said with a sly, amused expression, "my wife and staff call me "Horry." Now I know you all have excellent vocabularies, as our testing showed. My nickname is spelled H-o-r-r-y, not h-o-a-r-y, meaning extremely old. I'm fifty-nine, if you care to know," he added, his smile widening. "Good luck to you all." He turned and walked off-stage, followed by his four chiefs.

The four guides rose from their front-row seats. One after the other, each called out a list of six names. Leo took his place in the fourth group. *We're being separated by gender,* he realized. *Maybe more candidates are coming this afternoon.*

"Hello, Group Four, I'm Zeke Adamly, your guide." Despite Zeke's down-home name, he sported a gold-buttoned navy blazer, pressed khakis, and striped tie as if he'd just left his Ivy League campus. He ushered them into an elevator that took them to the third floor, where the rear doors opened to a glass wall. Leo could see the other three groups farther down the long corridor.

"To your right and behind you are the residences and common areas. To your left and behind you are the classrooms and lecture halls," proclaimed Zeke. But everyone's attention was fixated on the three-story view beyond the glass in front of them. "Gentlemen, you are looking at the stations of your future. Directly in front of you is the Cradle Station with its four rows of ten individual cradles. Each of you will be assigned a cradle of your own. This is where you will be prepared for your subzero experience."

"Preparation? What exactly does that entail?" asked one of the candidates.

"Good question. A system of intravenous tubes will be attached to your bodies so that various nutrients, emollients and hydrating agents can reach their targeted destinations," said Zeke. "For example, oxygenated nutrients are perfused to the capillaries via one of the tubes. Cryoprotectants help stop cell shrinkage, dehydration and toxicity. You will also be wired so that our staff can monitor all aspects of your instillation process."

"Dr Richards promised it wouldn't be rigorous or painful," a shaky voice popped up.

"And it won't be—because you will be anaesthetized beforehand," responded Zeke.

"Doesn't look like there's much privacy out there," added yet another tense voice.

"You'll be attended to one at a time, so privacy won't be an issue," Zeke said. "At the end of your Cradle Station period you will be moved to the Clinical Station."

The group followed him for some thirty feet. He stopped and turned to face them. "At the Clinical Station your metabolic heart rate, organ function tempo, and electrocardiac activity will be chemically slowed until they're barely detectable. Then your cradle will be sealed. A gas with ultra-cold quantum capabilities will slowly replace the air you breathe. Next, your body temperature will be lowered in miniscule stages while your body fluids are exchanged for a nonfreezing, paste-like soup that is forced or perfused through your body under pressure. Everything the body needs is provided without the body having to process it. As the body temperature approaches the initial freeze point, the temperature will suddenly be dropped well below freezing to avoid ice damage to the vital organs."

They followed Zeke to view the Deep-Freeze Station. He pointed  to several enormous cranes. "A crane's job is to lift the cradle out of its gurney bed, orient it in a vertical or standing position, raise it high over one of those large stainless containers on wheels and lower it inside for the duration. The containers are called Thermo-Kettles."

"Look more like missile silos to me," said Leo with a nervous chuckle.

Zeke gave him an annoyed look, choosing to ignore the oddly accurate observation. "The Thermo-Kettle has all the necessary pumps, machinery and parallel interconnects the individual cradle has. Each Thermo-Kettle will accommodate four cryonauts. Once all the connections are transferred, the temperature is dropped incrementally with nitrogen to the terminal temperature: minus 139 degrees Centigrade or minus 77 degrees on the absolute Kelvin scale."

The group stared in awe at the monumental, massive structures.

"Now follow me," said Zeke, walking briskly to what he called the Monitoring Station. "Here we keep an eye on the Thermo-Kettles for about a week before moving them to The Farm."

"Just what is The Farm?" a voice interjected. "And where is it located?"

Before Zeke could answer, another candidate piped up. "Does that mean we're being put out to pasture?" Tentative giggles rippled through the group.

Zeke raised an eyebrow and pressed his lips together to suppress his irritation. He knew he should chill out a little himself, but being a "people person" just wasn't in him—even now when the candidates' anxieties were obvious and to be expected. He pressed on. "Try to imagine forty or more of these Thermo-Kettles lined up in rows and columns like crops in the field. Get the image? The Farm is a special facility large enough to house and caretake hundreds and possibly thousands of Thermo-Kettles. Each one will be monitored precisely. A touch of nitrogen will be added here and there to maintain frozen status. Also, very important, an occasional recharge of nutrients and the like will keep the bodies vital."

"Who watches this farm to see that nothing goes wrong?" asked Leo.

"That's a fair question," Zeke finally conceded. "Highly trained scientists watch the monitors and administer any replenishment necessary. Three eight-hour shifts, day in and day out. A second crew takes over on alternate weeks. A medical doctor and an advanced-practice registered nurse check in regularly and are always on call. There are backup systems at every station, so it is unlikely that anything would go wrong."

"Who's paying for all this expensive upkeep, and how do we know if they will keep on paying once we're in la-la land?" Leo asked.

Zeke's officious manner thawed a little. Leonard Tall-Chief's keen mind was not to be ignored. "Not to worry. The program is fully funded from start to finish for 600 cryonauts over the next hundred years, so if you're not resuscitated before then, you will be at the end of ninety-nine years. Private donations have been matched by government monies to create the Principal Cryonautics Fund or PCF. The program will operate on the interest the principal fund generates. The Federal Government guarantees the interest rate, so we won't run out of money. Does that answer your question?"

"Yeah," said Leo. "It's sort of like having a ninety-nine-year lease on the likes of us."

Several in the group murmured "Uh-huh," but without humor. It all sounded quite preposterous. One skeptic piped up in a taunting tone, "Yeah, sure, like nothing's going to go wrong in ninety-nine years."

"These are legitimate questions and answers, and they're not to be taken lightly," retorted Zeke, the hairs on his neck rising as he skated on thin factual ice. "We're talking about your lives here. It's proven  technology, but we haven't the long-term experience to say that absolutely nothing can go wrong."

"You make it sound like we're already on our way to the grave," said Leo. "Can't we lighten up a bit?"

"If you want to be the class clown, have it your way," Zeke retorted, wishing he'd never taken this job at Hybernautics. He led them from the glass-lined corridor into the classroom area, where they found a mockup cradle for them to examine up close. The clear top was open, so each candidate had a chance to check out the interior. Leo took his turn feeling the padded linings and looking for nonexistent controls.

"Not exactly built for comfort, is it?" he asked. "Hey, I'm six-foot-four and 240 pounds. Is this thing going to be big enough for me? And how do you drive it? Where are the controls?"

"We can accommodate seven-foot, 280-pound cryonauts in a few of the cradles," replied Zeke. "But where do you think you're going? There are no controls. You are traveling through time, Mr. Tall-Chief—not space, and you'll be in no shape to maneuver anything by the time the lid is dropped on your cradle. You will be comfortably asleep—until our medical and scientific staff resuscitate you."

The cold, blunt facts hovered over the now-silent group. It would be difficult for them to digest the idea that this was much more than putting your head down for one night's sleep. The lying down was complicated. But what of the awakening?

Zeke pointed out all the latest in audio and visual aids and listed some of the topics they would be learning. He then led them down the residential corridor, dropping each of the cryonauts off at their respective windowless residences for the next three weeks. They were instructed to immediately strip, shower and don the clothing laid out on the bed. Classes would start the next morning.

Leo found the shower pleasant and relaxing, and the white pullover top with matching no-belt slacks fit him amazingly well. The room was furnished in stark modern—black, white and chrome. He tried the queen-size bed and found the mattress to his liking. He flipped on the fifty-inch television screen, larger than any he'd ever been able to afford, and settled into the inviting recliner; it smelled of new expensive leather. His heartbeat slowly returned to near-normal.

Chapter 6

## Instillation

(November 2059)

**A**T THE END OF THE SECOND WEEK OF CLASSES, on a Thursday, Leo received a note from Zeke. "Congratulations, Leonard Tall-Chief, you have successfully completed all your training. Report for instillation at seven sharp Saturday morning after a shower and fresh clothes. You are to eat nothing on Friday and expect to undergo an enema at day's end." Leo wondered why Zeke hadn't approached him personally with such big news, but soon his thoughts drifted elsewhere. He really didn't care what Zeke thought of him. He'd probably never see him again.

On Friday Leo tried to relax by reading, but he couldn't concentrate on his Isaac Asimov novel. He tossed it on the table and surrendered to watching TV movies for most of the day. As a man with a normally voracious appetite, it was difficult to think about anything but food, especially in the late evening. His prominent aquiline nose inhaled the aromas of all three meals wafting toward him from the dining room down the hall. That was more frustrating than satisfying.

He also knew the enema would be unpleasant, but Friday night proved even more fitful. He'd turned in early, thinking a night's sleep would do him some good, but lying there sweating on top of the sheets, he saw the folly in his reasoning—sleep was the least of his worries. Brooding on the prospect of his daring journey through time, he asked himself again and again: *Have I made the right choice?*

At last, Saturday morning wriggled, squeezed and struggled its way out of the night's prolonged darkness. Leo showered, dressed and reported to the Cradle Station on the dot of seven as instructed. He was greeted by a doctor and two technicians, all garbed in what appeared to be hazmat outfits sans headgear. Leo recognized the two technicians as Elaine and Brad. They had been instructors at some point in his training He noticed that Elaine's long, shiny blonde hair had been tucked into the collar of her white hazmat ensemble. Aside from the bulky garb, Leo found she wasn't unattractive. He acknowledged her ten-dollar smile and turned his attention to the balding, gray-bearded doctor, who was beginning to show his impatience.

Dr. Obermeyer checked Leo's vital signs and found everything within their acceptable limits. With the stethoscope finally back around his neck, he made a request that startled Leo. "Now, young man, if you'll remove all of your clothes, please."

The embarrassed Leo shot a glance at Elaine, who stared blankly off into space, and then complied. "Am I to travel though time in my birthday suit?" he asked as she took his khakis, polo shirt, briefs, socks and shoes from him. "This outfit isn't very stylish anyway," he added. When none of his nervous antics elicited the slightest smile, he decided it was better to keep quiet. He stood still, arms crossed over his private parts, shivering. But keeping quiet didn't last long. "Why is it so damned cold in here? Is this a torture chamber? Have you guys started freezing me already?"

"As to your first question, yes. You will be traveling through time naked," said Dr. Fred. "If you had paid attention to your class work, Leo, you would know all these answers. Your bare body will make it easier to accommodate the many medical and physiological monitoring connections that will accompany you on your journey. Trendy clothes don't fit in with our goals. The temperature in here is kept at 10 degrees Celsius—that's 50 degrees Fahrenheit—to limit the bacterial count."

"Step in front of the screen, please," said Brad, as he pointed to a ten-foot-high stainless steel half-cylinder, standing on end. "You are going to be sprayed with an antibacterial, sterilizing agent. But first, let's do this." He lowered a helmet, similar to a hazmat helmet, over Leo's head. That done, Brad attached a nozzle to a hose, and pulled the nozzle's trigger.

By this time Leo realized that the three staff members had also donned their protective headgear. He suddenly felt the cool, damp draft of the spray covering his body from his neck down. Then he heard, "Arms away from your body…Turn, please." He raised both arms, pivoted, and felt the spray again. Leo sensed the pressured air covering his body's backside, leaving him with even more of a chill. "Turn back, please." The air poured over him once more.

"You're scrubbed clean now, Leo. You can exit the sterilizer," said Brad after removing Leo's headgear.

Leo stepped away from the cylinder, shivering and shaking in his altogether. He clutched both upper arms across his chest, but even that didn't help.

When the heavy, odorless, antibacterial dust had finally settled, Leo saw that the others had removed their own headgear. Leo watched Elaine disappear into a room about thirty yards off to the right. Huge, automatic double doors bore a sign lettered in gold: Cradle Station. Moments later, the doors opened once again and she emerged rolling a long gurney toward him, completely covered by a clear plastic bubble. Leo's heart jumped a painful beat. His determination not to show his anxiety evaporated. "That sure as hell doesn't look like any cradle I've ever seen. Of course, not being a dad, what do I know?" he joked.

Elaine nodded, eyeing him with a sympathetic hint of a smile. "I know. It's a lot to take in," she said as she took in his powerful shoulders and washboard abs.

Elaine and Brad unlocked the clips holding the bubble cover in place, hefted it up and off the gurney and stowed it along one wall. Leo, still chilled miserably to the bone, sucked in his breath as he studied the contraption. "Cradle" was indeed a misnomer. It had no raised sides that one could feel cozy within. It appeared to be no more than a vinyl mattress, only a few inches thick, covering a gurney at least seven feet long,

Elaine lowered the gurney to its limit and motioned to him to approach it.

"Sit down," Brad commanded.

Leo lowered himself onto the mattress, which turned out to be at least room temperature, slightly more friendly to his backside.  His eyes fixed on a steel side table, where the doctor was fiddling with a clutter of paraphernalia. Leo saw several IV bottles, some filled with nearly clear contents, others containing darker liquids; enough tubing to fill a large suitcase; and an assortment of needles, valves and metering devices.

"Lie down, please," Elaine ordered. She stepped close, intending to push him onto his back—close enough for him to sniff any perfume. Leo eagerly inhaled. She wore none. Elaine was as sterile as their lab surroundings. Under other circumstances, he would've gotten aroused, but not here. His self-conscious nakedness was displaced by her now clinical manner—all business as she lifted both his strong, heavy legs up at once and swung them around onto the cradle. Brad joined her as they strapped each one down. The wrists and chest were next.

Although the few inches of padding afforded some little comfort, his physique soon settled through to the hard surface beneath. Even strapped down, Leo rocked side to side as he tried to find a comfort zone. "Any chance I can be upgraded to first class?" he blurted out, breaking his own promise to stop wise-cracking.

"Damn it, man, lie still," demanded an impatient, humorless Dr. Fred. "Just a small prick and we'll soon have you on your way."

Stunned by the doctor's vehemence and animosity, Leo looked away and stared at the two-story ceiling above him. He hardly noticed the pin prick and needle insertion, but within minutes, he felt a warm liquid sensation surging through his whole system. His stomach fought back a nauseated stirring, his mind a rush of angst. He wanted to say something more. The words actually reached his lips, but the only sounds he heard were from those around him. He thought he heard his own heart, and that seemed to beat slower and softer until not at all. The ceiling became less clear, so he tried to blink and found he couldn't. His eyes went blank on their own, not even registering the blackness that had taken over. He sensed he was falling, tumbling through nothingness—and then unaware of anything at all. As Leo lost consciousness, there was no way he could comprehend all that was happening to him. The IV had done its job and could now be removed and sealed off.

Brad appeared on the scene pushing a portable suspension support console containing cycling pumps, fluid and gas reservoirs, and electronic monitoring screens. He skillfully coupled it to the gurney, so console and gurney would move one behind the other like train cars. The technician then made all of the electrical, hydraulic and pneumatic connections between the portable console and the cradle.

Once they had determined that Leo could sense nothing more, Dr. Obermeyer and his two capable technicians continued to establish the myriad connections between man and machine. Perfusion tubes protruded from the chest's cardiac region. A maze of wires was interlaced between the cradle and console. Electrodes were attached by suction cups to nearly every part of Leo's body. The pumps were started, and the monitoring circuits were energized within a matter of seconds after connection. Soon all body activity had been bypassed, retired and replaced by the console machinery. A thick, oxygen-rich preservation soup flowed through Leo's body, carrying with it a polar aprotic agent. This agent, with its excess hydrogen protons—along with other cryoprotectants— prevented organ damage during the anti-vitrification process, the avoidance of ice while entering the subfreezing zones.

Brad and Elaine lugged the bubble canopy back to the gurney, attached it to an overhead crane and lowered it over the cradle. One by one, the forty-eight surrounding latches were locked down to ensure a full pressure seal. Slowly, a yellowish gas containing yet another polar aprotic agent replaced the air inside the canopy. At this point nitrogen and another gas, capable of ultra-cold quantum qualities, entered the canopy, slowly dropping the temperature inside to just above the freezing point. Suddenly, an increased flow of pure nitrogen pushed the temperature well below freezing: a quick freeze to prevent dreaded ice formations that would make organs brittle, excessively fragile, and subject to rupture. More nitrogen, and the temperature dropped quickly and continuously to stabilize at minus 139 degrees Celsius. There, at the ideal temperature for the suspension of life, the flow of nitrogen was curtailed to maintenance levels—with an additional shot of coolant available when needed.

Dr. Obermeyer, Elaine and Brad monitored every aspect of instillation repeatedly over the next four hours, especially checking for leaks. Satisfied with a successful instillation, Brad hitched a tiny tractor to the two-car train and drove it to the Deep-Freeze station, where the Thermo-Kettles stood ready to receive the cryonauts. He stopped at Kettle Twelve. It loomed ten feet tall and twelve feet wide, gleaming stainless steel. Kettle Twelve was tagged specifically for four cradles, one assigned to Leonard Tall-Chief. Brad uncoupled the cradle from both the tractor and the trailing console and hooked the cradle's head loop to an overhead crane. The crane's control pad enabled him to bring the cradle to a vertical— on end—position, where he and Elaine made parallel connections between the cradle and the Thermo-Kettle lid.

Having completed and inspected all the tube and cable connections, Brad used the crane to boost the cradle above the Thermo-Kettle and then lower it into one of four chambers inside. Transfer valves and switches permitted him to shift all of the console functions to the larger kettle systems. Once all the transfers had been made, he sealed the portable console's connection ports and removed the associated tubes and cabling. This procedure enabled him to close and seal the kettle chamber lid. The operation's final step was to add Leo's laminated file and picture to the kettle's breast-plate document holder. One of the four chambers was now full. The crew was done for the morning.

* * * *

**M**arian Mapleton, making her daily trip to the mailbox at the curb, discovered an official-looking thick letter. She hurried into the house, and from the front hall yelled up the stairs. "Fanny, there's a letter for you. Looks important."

"Who's it from?"

"I don't know. It has a strange logo and no return address."

Fanny clattered down the uncarpeted stairs, took the letter from her mother, and ripped it open. "It's from those suspended-animation people, Hybernautics."

Marian's face blanched. "Honey, I thought all that lottery business ended a month ago."

"So did I," said Fanny as she read each word of the letter twice. "It seems the program ran out of cryonaut alternates who have Infirenza, so they drew my name. I'm supposed to report to a Chicago address at eight on Monday morning."

"Oh, no! Sweetheart, are you sure you want to go through with this?"

"After what I went through with last week's fever I'm willing to try anything. I have to go, Mom. The fever's getting higher and more intense every day. Pretty soon the fits will be getting closer and closer. I won't be able to take much more."

"Maybe it won't come back again," said Marian, the age lines in her face deepening as she spoke.

"Yeah, sure, Mom. The disease has a hold on me for sure. The scientists are nowhere with their research for a cure—let alone parceling out any cure for the likes of me."

"But sweetie, I can't guarantee that I'll still be living when they wake you up in the future."

Fanny's intense green eyes filled with tears. She blinked hard to keep from crying in front of her mother. "Jeez, Mom, that's the only part I'm having trouble digesting. I can't imagine life without you. There's nobody else I give a hoot for. There's never been anyone else special in my life." She carefully avoided bringing up the perpetual regret that both she and her mother shared. Her father had callously taken off and never returned when she was only a month old. "And you know what else, Mom? I'm twenty-two and I've never had sex! If I had a boyfriend maybe this cryogenics mission would be a lot harder."

Marian took the unsurprising revelation in stride. "I'm so sorry, dear. But weren't you excited about that young Native American man you met when you registered for this suspended animals program?"

"Animation, Mom. Suspended animation. Yeah, he was a hunk. His name was Leo. I wish he'd asked me out."

"Maybe he'll be in the program, too."

"There's no way of knowing, Mom."

Marian was out of ideas. "Can I at least help you with the packing?"

Fanny shook her unruly blonde curls. "There's actually no packing to be done. I'm to show up with the clothes on my back and my driver's license. That's it. *Finis.*"

"But how are you going to get there, dear?" Marian had one final hope that this obstacle would keep her home.

"They've included an airline ticket and boarding pass. A bus will meet me and take me to their facilities." Fanny's words caught in her throat. "I'm a grown woman and I'm still scared."

"I don't blame you, sweetheart. I'd be a mess. In fact, I'm already a mess." She embraced her daughter and hugged her tightly in desperation for several minutes.

* * * *

**B**efore finishing her first week of training in Chicago, Fanny learned that the woman she had replaced had committed suicide when the Infirenza fevers overtook her one night after classes. Fanny put the news out of her mind.

## Unto the Third Generation

* * * *

Thirty days passed and three of the other Thermo-Kettle chambers still had not been filled. On the forty-third day that situation changed. Francine Mapleton, a star pupil and compliant patient, was installed in the second chamber of Kettle Twelve. The other two chambers remained empty. On the seventy-third day, Kettle Twelve was transferred to the Kettle Farm for long-term cryosuspension.

The would-be friends, Francine Mapleton and Leonard Tall-Chief, were now only a few feet away from each other and yet worlds apart.

* * * *

Chapter 7

# Ebb and Flow
### (The year 2071)

THE RAGING INFIRENZA EPIDEMIC HAD BEGUN TO subside in 2064. The newer cases were less severe, and by 2068, no new cases were even reported. In a few of the milder cases, the patients even managed to survive. Although no effective cure had been found, mankind's future had somehow become more viable, at least for the time being. As a result, the third cryonaut launch was deemed unnecessary.

Horry Richards leaned back in his swivel chair, shifting his weight to adjust for his chronically sore lower back, and stared at the ceiling. He heard a knock at the door. "Come in," he said. The now seventy-year-old CEO slowly straightened up and pulled his keyboard closer. He wanted to look productive.

"Good to see you, Marie, have a seat. The others should be along shortly."

In a matter of minutes the five senior members of his staff surrounded his teak power desk. Marie Fontaine, Jon Seward, Ernest Baer and Fred Obermeyer sat opposite him. At the far end, but closest to Horry, sat Ellen May Richards, his wife and now comptroller of Hybernautics. Horry had placed her in this position at the insistence of his mother-in-law, an aggressive, voluble majority stockholder. The truth was, Ellen reveled in her job; it gave her the authority to apply the principles she'd learned in acquiring her MBA. To her husband's secret joy, she had much less time to fritter away their personal wealth.

Horry called the meeting to order. "Everyone, I've gathered you together for some important decisions today. We are under a great deal of pressure from the Principal Cryonautics Fund. It's 2071 and nearly four years since the last new case of Infirenza was reported. Now that the disease is no longer a threat, the PCF's Board of Directors is looking to commence cryogenic distillations. To put it bluntly, they plan to dissolve the preservation fund—meaning, they are pressing forward to kill our program. Apparently, they feel there are more important uses for their money. I must agree." Horry peered at each of them through his horn-rimmed glasses to gauge their reaction. "It's high time we resuscitated these brave pioneers and restored them to their rightful lives. Personally, I'd like to get started as soon as possible and complete the restorations quickly—several at a time, if necessary."

"This is not something to be rushed into," said Fred. "There are many factors to be considered here. Mainly, we do not have a lot of experience in cryogenic distillation. Each of the cryonauts may present unique problems. In the past we've encountered confusion, memory loss, and even permanent brain damage." Not to mention the two first-group deaths, which he decided not to bring up.

Jon leaped in to disagree with Fred. "Chief, we've already anticipated the mental problems. I plan to hire temporary experts: one or two additional psychiatrists and three or four psychologists to handle them. We've also commandeered space in the trainee living areas for the recovery acclimation process. We can handle a number of revivals at a time."

Fred protested. "But we've also found several cases of physical deterioration in other organs. I propose that we conduct the distillations slowly, carefully and serially so that those who are distillated later can benefit from what we learn from the earliest ones revived."

A cloud of annoyance crossed Horry's face. "Deterioration? What kind of physical deterioration are we talking about here?"

"Offhand," said Fred, "I can think of severe damage from dehydration. Organ tissue decay, cell shrinkage, and even some toxicity."

Ellen rapped sharply on the desk with her gold pen to get their attention. "Shouldn't we be willing to accept some collateral losses and impairments in these cases? It might be simpler and cheaper to just pay out their insurance claims, rather than tie up much-needed funds for any extended period. I'm with my husband on this thing."

Horry squirmed in his chair and remained silent. He was at a loss to respond to his wife's cold-hearted suggestions.

"Ellen! I might get fired for saying this," started Ernest, "but, damn it, you should be ashamed of yourself to think of people—no, brave pioneers risking their lives for science—as merely accounting figures in your friggin' corporate books. I helped train these people and got to know them. I have feelings for them. And even if I didn't, I wouldn't want them on my conscience. No! I'm afraid I'm solidly with Fred on this one."

"Well, aren't you a pushover," sneered Ellen. "You can get as emotional as you want, Ernie, but it's not going to fly with the PCF. They want out—now."

Horry winced. His lower back spasmed. "Take it easy, Ernie, you're not fired," he said. "That's quite a speech, but I think you ought to display a little more respect for my wife."

"Boss, it was not my intent to disrespect anyone, only I can't abide that kind of callous opportunism. These people's lives are at stake."

"What about you, Marie?" asked Fred.

"I'm a mathematician. I deal with numbers, mainly statistics, all the time," she said, nervously fingering the collar of her silk blouse. "Sometimes they're about technical products and sometimes they're about people and their opinions. I rarely see those faces or hear their voices or know of their contributions to society. But one thing I do know is that I wish to lead a righteous and ethical life." Marie spoke in a soft but firm voice. "I would not like to have these cryonauts on my conscience. I will not condone anything but the most careful and advantageous procedures during revival. They're deserving of our very best."

"Jeez, Chief," began Jon, "I've developed a conscience on this, too. Fred and the others have made some good points. I would expect the specialists I'm hiring to come with the same sensitivity."

"In that case, I think I'll have to go along with you on that," said Horry. "You've convinced me that serial, careful distillation is the way to go."

"You mean you're going to cave to these wimps?" asked Ellen, her eyes hard as her lacquered nails.

"I'm not caving, Ellen. They're right," replied Horry. "A good tort lawyer could tear a huge chunk out of our assets, in addition to the money we'll lose from the PCF. The matter is settled."

"Okay, Boss, then where do we start?" asked Ernie.

"Don't you mean who do we start with?" corrected Marie.

"Yeah, Boss, that's what I meant—who?" said Ernie.

"How about Group III, the big donors first," suggested Ellen. "Those whose families funded and made a large chunk of our program possible. They might be grateful enough to remember us favorably in the future."

"No, I don't think so," said Horry. "Fred, tell me if I'm wrong. Aren't the first ones the most risky, the most likely to wind up with the biggest problems?"

"You're absolutely right, Horry."

"We could reverse the order and take the donors last," offered Jon.

"The only way to be fair would be by lots," said Marie. "Put all the names in the proverbial jar and draw them one-by-one until the facility is cleared."

Horry looked around the table at all the nodding heads and

declared, "That's settled. Marie, you can handle the lottery."

"All the names?" asked Ernest.

"Why not?" said Horry. "We're trying to be fair and soothe all our consciences here."

Ernie's freckled face paled. "You're forgetting: we have two advanced cases of Infirenza in cold storage. For them it has to be a medical decision. Infirenza is far too virulent a disease to risk bringing back a potential carrier, let alone a pair of them. Besides, no cure has been found for them yet."

"Ahem!" said Ellen, pointedly clearing her throat. "Don't you see? You do have a legitimate excuse to pull the plug—at least on those two."

"Ellen! I won't hear any more of that nonsense." Horry could see he had planted fire in his spouse's eyes. He knew there would be hell to pay for it later.

"Then what do you plan on doing with them?" asked Jon.

"Marie," Horry ordered, "exclude those two from your lottery. We'll deal with them at some later time."

"Horry!" challenged Ellen. "You mean you would tie up a whole multibillion-dollar Kettle Farm facility just for those two? Now that's fiscally irresponsible."

Horry paused, squinting, pondering. "Hmm, I think the PCF board might agree with you there, dear." He looked around the table. "Any suggestions, colleagues?"

"We could move that one kettle to a smaller facility," said Fred.

"A ludicrous idea," retorted Horry. "How can we support an isolated kettle outside of its farm?"

"There are several portable support consoles in the labs," replied Ernest. "Those five machines have been idle for years, but they can easily be brought up to snuff for the job. Besides, we're going to need a couple of them anyway for distillation. All we'll need then is a supply of nitrogen and the sustenance soup we use in the perfusion process."

"How about cutting staff?" asked Jon. "We've got almost

two dozen employees operating the farm now. We should be able to cut that figure significantly. Say, three or four technicians, maybe a physicist and a medical doctor."

"That sound reasonable," Horry said. "Pretty workable, in fact. If not, we can make adjustments later. Fred? How soon can we get started?"

"A few days to prep the equipment. A week to be sure we have the necessary supplies. Maybe a week from Monday. That soon enough for everyone?"

Horry polled the faces around the room and counted the nods. He ignored Ellen's reaction: her full red lips compressed in a pout. "Sounds like we have a plan, ladies and gentlemen. Any questions or comments?"

"When do we move the Infirenza two?" asked Jon.

"When all the other distillations have been completed," said Horry. "Any more comments?"

There were none. The staff dispersed.

* * * *

**S**oon afterward, the cryogenic distillations began. One by one, the pioneers were brought back—that is, all but poor Leo and Fanny. But the process that had appeared to be a no-brainer was not smooth sailing. One cryonaut died from brain damage. One suffered total memory loss. Three suffered partial memory loss. And six others experienced severe organ deficiencies. Horry Richards and his staff played down the casualties and labeled the cryogenic suspension program a qualified success. After all, these cryonauts had survived a record twelve years of preservation. The last of the thirty-eight cryonauts were serially distilled in October of 2071.

At last Ellen May Richards had her way. Much of the Principal Cryonautics Fund was diverted to her own pet projects.

* * * *

**E**very one of the returned men and women—despite any disabilities—indulged in the synthetic groceries called Synthomanna. And why not? It had been a universal success. The food was healthy, low-calorie, attractive and delicious. Even a dental additive, an advanced form of fluoride, had found its way into the recipe lot, so that dental health had improved significantly.

Kettle Twelve, containing just Leo and Fanny, was moved to a small facility in northern Minnesota. It had minimal security, fewer backup support systems, and less oversight. The isolated facility was named the Pucevale Kettle Farm after a small nearby town. At the Principal Cryonauts Fund, talk of pulling the plug arose frequently for political and financial expediency. Out of pure loyalty Horry intervened to keep Kettle Twelve going. The smaller farm's expenditures became nearly invisible at the corporate level, and soon the pair were forgotten altogether in the boardroom.

Fanny and Leo remained oblivious, of course, to both the politics and the geographic changes that were destined to radically affect them.

Chapter 8

# Distillation
(The years 2077 through 2084)

THE YEAR 2077 DAWNED WITH A MEDICAL miracle. Scientists discovered a cure for Infirenza. They successfully isolated the superbug at the heart of the evil, intractable disease. Months later, they developed a remarkable new antibiotic that effectively annihilated Infirenza in a matter of a few days. They called it the Winslow antibiotic, for Wilhelmina Winslow, the scientist who led the research. The unfortunate remaining survivors, who continued to be plagued by their recycling lesser symptoms, served as voluntary guinea pigs. The prompt disappearance of their symptoms offered proof that the disease had been licked once and for all. Universal joy and celebration greeted the formerly afflicted patients. The wiping out of the Infirenza pandemic, coupled with the successful conquering of global hunger, brought a wave of unprecedented optimism to every nation.

* * * *

**A** few hundred thousand did not eat the miracle food, for various reasons. Remote, primitive and isolated societies had no knowledge of, or access to, Synthomanna. Others knew of it but preferred to remain loyal to traditional foods. These were the skeptics, the naysayers; among them, many farmers, vegans, vegetarians, restaurateurs, anti-preservative individuals, and some of the outright wealthy.

Nevertheless, the media trumpeted the best news yet. Any illnesses attributed to malnutrition or food-related disorders had completely disappeared. Apparently, no one had developed any allergies or noticeable impairment from Synthomanna.

Until 2079.

In January of that year Dr. Angeline Terracie, an American scientist, made an appalling discovery. The third-generation consumers of Synthomanna were experiencing a sharply dwindling birth rate. Dr. Terracie, an internationally acclaimed nutrition expert, determined that the dropping birth rate was directly related to the miracle food. At least half a dozen research teams around the world spent the next six months verifying and validating her horrific findings. The world population was in trouble once again.

* * * *

**O**n April 12th, 2084, a nurse practitioner and a physician at Pucevale Kettle Farms in upper Minnesota were making their routine rounds. Kitty Fairfield and Dr. Marc Litton had just begun their 4 a.m. to 12 noon shifts. Their critical responsibility was to check on the status of the two frozen residents: Leonard and Francine. Were their support systems functioning properly? So far, each day, yes. Then Marc would leave for his patient rounds at the local hospital, where he was a second-year resident in cardiology. Kitty would continue her shift alone. Bundled in parkas, the temperature in the mid-thirties, they walked briskly; the sun wouldn't be up for another three hours. Marc sometimes wondered why Kitty wanted this job when she could be in a professional practice of her own. After all, she had impressive credentials as an APRN, an advanced-practice registered nurse with a master's degree. Now he was to find out that she had a deeply humanitarian side and surprising spirit of adventure.

Tall, lanky Kitty was in a talkative mood. "Ever wonder who these two popsicles were when they were alive?"

"Not really," said Marc. Only five-foot-five, he had to take two steps to each of her long strides. "As far as I'm concerned, it's a good paying job. I'm babysitting a twelve-foot chunk of steel. I check, appraise and record the readings on all the gauges and meters every hour. If any of them need refreshment or a change of filters, I'm there for them. It's like I'm giving Kettle Twelve a bottle and changing its diapers. I can't bring myself to feel for the damn thing."

Kitty cocked her head. Her chestnut-brown hair, in a clipped pixie cut with bangs, made her look younger than thirty-one. "Babysitting? You're a doctor. Don't you care at all about the two real people inside?"

Tightening the knot in his tie, Marc gave her a sidelong glance. "The people I care about are my heart patients in the hospital. They're the real people—awaiting surgery or in recovery, depending on my judgment, my decisions."

"But these two in the kettle. Haven't you ever looked at their pictures? They're both quite attractive, don't you think?"

"Attractive? Well, yeah," Marc conceded. "But they're not exactly alive, are they?"

"They're not exactly dead either," claimed Kitty. "They could be distilled and resuscitated at any time just like the other thirty-eight cryonauts."

"I suppose so," he said, "except for the fact that they've been sentenced to 'Indefinite distillation.' Haven't you noticed that yellow stamp on both their files?"

"Of course, Marc, and frankly, it scares me. I see it all the time, but I wonder why the Hybernautics Board hasn't rescinded their decision and resuscitated them now that a cure for Infirenza has been found."

Marc shrugged. "Don't know. Maybe it's something political or maybe those in charge have forgotten all about these two poor slobs. Why are you so interested in their extended welfare all of a sudden?"

Kitty took her time replying. "When was the last time you even thought about having sex?"

"My, aren't we getting personal," Marc said, his sharp features breaking into a sly grin. "You got something in mind?" For a split second he imagined climbing on top of her in bed and he actually felt a spark of heat in his groin. Just as quickly, it evaporated. "If you must know, it's been years. And it's the same for everyone on this planet—at least everyone who's been consuming that synthetic junk food. Are you any different?"

"Of course not," Kitty said. "I've stopped eating the crazy Synthomanna stuff just like everyone else under the age of seventy." With a second master's in the health sciences, she routinely studied the technical journals. "From what I've read, the experts differ. Some believe Synthomanna is actually causing sterilization. Others think it's suppressing the sex drive. But if the suppression theory is right, I wonder—suppose it has to do with only the male or only the female libido, not both?"

"What are you getting at, Kitty?"

They had just arrived in front of Kettle Twelve. She flicked on her Maglite and pointed its powerful beam at the large laminated photograph of Leonard Tall-Chief nailed to the front of the kettle. "You've got to admit he's one hell of a handsome, rugged, virile-looking hunk. And he was instilled before Synthomanna was widely available." Kitty smiled for the first time that morning. "Suppose it's the male drive that's in question. He'd be a great one to experiment with."

"So would she," Marc joked. "For the sake of science, of course. Wait! You're not thinking of resuscitating both of them on our own?"

"I'm thinking about it."

"And without direct orders from Hybernautics, girl?"

"Why not?"

"You realize we could both lose our jobs for insubordination."

"Well, Marc, if we resuscitated them, the farm would have no residents, and there would be no reason for us to be here. The company would save thousands of dollars."

"What makes you think we could resuscitate them on our

own, anyway?" he asked.

"Hey, Doctor, don't forget, we're experts. The two of us took part in more than twenty other distillations. What makes you think we couldn't do this?"

"What if we run into physiological or psychological complications?" he asked. "What then?"

"Come on, Marc. We both have the essential tools. I've even had four additional years of Army field experience. I think, between us, we can handle anything physiological—that is, within reason. If there's a psychological problem, there'd be time to call someone in."

"It's that 'within reason' part that bothers me," he emphasized. "Why take such a risk? Why jeopardize our employment and our reputations, our futures? Where's the reward?"

"The reward?" Her assertive alto voice rose with excitement. "We would get credit for helping to restart the human race. It's a gigantic throw of the dice, of course. It's possible that neither one of us will connect successfully, physically, with our counterpart in the kettles. Still, bringing the two of them together just might get human sexuality back on track. I don't know about you, but I miss having sex, and this might be my last chance at it."

"Good God!" Marc said. A shiver of anxiety mixed with anticipation shot through his wiry body. "But it could be a serious risk—fame and fortune on the one hand; ruination and loss of my license to practice medicine on the other. Your credentials, too. Offhand, I'd say our chances are maybe eighty-twenty. And you're forgetting—these two have Infirenza. What if they transmit it to one or both of us? We don't want to be responsible for starting a whole new epidemic."

"Of course not," Kitty said. "I see one major obstacle: getting hold of the Winslow antibiotic."

"They're running some reverse engineering analyses in our pharmacology lab at my hospital this week. Maybe I could get some samples. Do we have everything else?"

Kitty felt a swell of excitement as her brain shifted into

overdrive. "We have their original blood, plus several matching pints frozen in reserve. All we need is the same machinery we used for instillation and support. We have the same time sequence and checklist we used for the other thirty-eight cryonauts back in Illinois. So what else is there? Are you with me, Marc?"

"Probably, but I want to sleep on it for a few days. First, let's see how accessible the antibiotic is."

* * * *

**O**n Saturday Marc phoned Kitty to say he wanted in. He was able to get the necessary doses of the Winslow antibiotic, but refused to say how he obtained them. They knew they would both be working a double shift to assure the safety of each patient. Four days later, they had assembled all the supplies they would need for the distillation and resuscitation of the two frozen cryonauts.

In April of 2084, the plan went into action. Leo and Fanny had been in suspension for twenty-four years, five months and twelve days. Kitty manipulated the overhead crane controls to lift the two cradles, one by one, out of Kettle Twelve. They were gently laid down in their horizontal positions.

When Marc arrived to do his part, he brought along a trusted colleague, an operating room nurse, to assist. The woman's name was Violet Zolan, and she was sworn to secrecy. She assisted Marc in his sterile scrub-up.

Resuscitation began with Leo.

At regular intervals, precisely manipulating the valves and other controls, Kitty released small amounts of nitrogen, allowing the temperature to rise incrementally. By 6 p.m. the temperature had risen sufficiently above the freezing point for the next step. She began diluting the heavier soup of suspension that had been perfused through Leo's system with oxygenated blood and nutrients. As the mixture thinned, she lessened the fluid pressure accordingly.

After the overall body temperature had stabilized at 10 degrees Celsius for at least two hours of thawing, Kitty, Marc and Violet removed the cradle canopy. Marc surgically opened Leo's central body cavity and sprayed a hydrating agent over the exposed organs and arteries to make them more pliable. By now, pure oxygenated blood and nutrients were coursing through Leo's arteries and veins all the way to the capillaries, and Marc had to preserve the precious cavity fluid with local clamps. Next, he surgically reconnected the aorta and ventricle to the heart, paralleling the machine's connections to those arteries. Afterward, he palpated the heart, lungs and surrounding areas to ensure pliability and check for hardening or rupturing.

Violet placed a breathing mask, connected to the portable console's respirator, over Leo's face. She fastened it tightly behind his head to form a solid seal. Marc slowly applied positive pressure to inflate Leo's flattened lungs. Kitty set the respirator machine to force breathing at regular intervals. All three of them watched as the lungs repeatedly filled to capacity and emptied thereafter. The weak adjoining muscles flexed with the machine's insistence.

Kitty rolled a cart that held a portable defibrillator up to Leo's cradle and handed the tiny paddle probes to Marc. She preset the panel dials to the prescribed initial values: a minimal amplitude voltage and short pulsewidth. The slow rise and fall of Leo's chest allowed for Marc's internal and direct access to the heart.

"Clear!" cried Marc, indicating that no one but the patient was a likely recipient of the charge.

Kitty depressed the DISCHARGE button on the panel, unleashing an amount of electricity that barely elicited a flex in Leo's heart. She readjusted the settings for a slightly more virulent delivery and waited the ten seconds for the next "Clear!" Kitty applied successively increasing charges in magnitude and width, along with sharper pulse slopes. The heart responded with stronger and stronger flexes until secondary, and even tertiary, flexing occurred from a single execution. They were getting close, like a car starting after a long period of disuse. Another shot. Leo's heart beat for two seconds—and then quit. One more shot, and his heart began pumping on its own. The three of them monitored the heart for the next half-hour to be sure.

Now, accepting the heart's reliability, Marc surgically dismantled the machine connections to the aorta and ventricle and sealed both accesses. Once he was convinced there were no leaks, he proceeded to suture the chest cavity closed. Violet reattached the external heart and brain probes to enable oscilloscope readouts for electrocardiograms (EKGs) and electroencephalographs (EEGs). The monitors on the portable console showed no anomalies.

Leo was left in that condition for the time being so they could turn their attention to Fanny. The entire procedure was repeated for her. Although no persisting physiological problems turned up, her EKG was a little irregular and slow to return within the expected bounds. Marc feared this might entail some short-term memory loss after resuscitation.

Leo and Fanny were left in their cradled gurneys until the end of the designated double shift. The regular-duty medical technicians on the succeeding shifts were informed of the patients' life changes and cautioned to keep the news of the covert distillation to themselves. Thrilled to take part in what appeared to be a proven success story, they agreed. The patients were later moved into comfortable hospital beds, but remained on artificial respiration for the next six days in order to build muscle strength and muscle memory. During that period they were still heavily sedated, fed intravenously, and drained with catheters. Marc dismissed Violet with his thanks and warned her again of the need for secrecy.

All that remained now was resuscitation.

Chapter 9

## Resuscitation
(The year 2084)

At THE END OF SIX DAYS MARC AND KITTY FELT their two cryonauts had spent sufficient time in the new hospital beds to rejuvenate and exercise all of their internal organs, muscles, and their innate neuro-messaging paths. To begin the actual revival, Marc administered a cautious dose of adrenaline to a central cardiac input line for each of them. Next, he attempted to remove the respirators to see if the patients could breathe on their own. Fanny did fine, but Leo needed an additional dose of adrenaline and an extra day on the respirator. After three more days of breathing successfully and independently, it was time for full resuscitation— time to awaken Leo and Fanny from more than a generation of supposedly restful sleep.

Today Kitty attached two electrical probes to Leo's temples and two more at key points on his scalp and forehead. Marc applied a preprogrammed series of electrical stimuli and viewed the repeating responses on the EEG monitor. He marked ten or twelve key nodes on the screen and printed out a stream of minor anomalies.

"This fellow is responding beautifully," declared Marc, his own heart quickening with excitement. "His brain is sharply attuned to the stimuli. I'll leave the program running in ninety-minute cycles until tomorrow morning."

"Are we sure enough?" Kitty asked. "I mean, has he responded enough for us to begin work on Fanny?"

"Yes. This young man should be ready for full revival tomorrow morning." Marc grinned. "What am I saying? This young man is technically older than I am. I'm twenty-eight. He's forty-seven."

Too focused to appreciate his joke, Kitty duplicated the arrangement of probes on Fanny and awaited Marc's okay to start the patient's preprogrammed stimuli. "Now?"

"Yes." Mark turned on the second stimulator and followed Fanny's results on a second EEG monitor. He cleared his throat and made a few other assorted noises while analyzing Fanny's resulting responses.

"Well?" Kitty asked.

"I think we've got another winner in our lady friend here."

* * * *

The next morning Kitty began incrementally cutting back the IV drip solution controlling the two patients' deep sedations— at a level close to bringing them out of their induced comas. She held Fanny's drip at that strength.

For Leo, she went farther, continuing to dilute his sedative until she noted occasional movement in his eyelids and tiny twitches of his fingers and lips. Hovering next to Kitty, Marc reached over and pulled back Leo's lids to shine a focused beam of light in each eye. Squinting at first, the eyes slowly relaxed into a floating daze, mesmerized by the optic intrusion.

"Ah-hah! We have contraction in both eyes, a good sign," Marc announced.

Eerily, the eyelids remained open and the exposed eyes followed the beam from side to side much as they should.

"And excellent eye movement and tracking as well," the doctor added.

Kitty reached out, taking hold of the hand with the twitching fingers, and massaged them with a paste of aloe mixed with aspirin. The fingers on that hand weakly folded around hers, approaching a sort of grip, perhaps an involuntary reflex, yet a partial confirmation of Leo's sensitivity to touch. When she looked up at him, she noted that his head had turned a bit and both his eyes stared back at her. Kitty smiled, and while she walked around the bed to massage the other hand, she kept a faithful watch on him. It wasn't until she reached the opposite side and had begun to work the other hand that his head moved in slight jerking motions to acknowledge what was happening over there. Leo was neither smiling nor frowning. Instead, he wore an expression of curiosity, then a sorrowful, lost-soul look—a look that changed to desperation.

Leo made a rasping, guttural sound, followed by aspirating and regurgitating the thick residue irritating his breathing path. As Kitty wiped the gooey stuff away, he coughed up more, with a few syllables and even a few recognizable words erupting from his throat. But none of it made any sense to the doctor and nurse.

"Better raise his head some," said Marc. He watched Kitty motor the top section of Leo's bedstead to a thirty-degree angle. "That's it. Let's see how the patient responds to a few more crude tests."

Marc clapped his hands sharply. Leo's head turned toward the source of the clatter. Marc cracked an ammonia ampoule and waved it under Leo's nose, causing a violent head jerk to escape the olfactory offense. Using an electric needle-like probe, Marc triggered a sharp, yet harmless, stimulus spark to key points as he explored Leo's limb extremities. Each pulsed spark was designed to not only elicit a particular muscular contraction, but educe an associated brain-activity response on the EEG recorder.

"Not bad," said Kitty. "Four out of the five senses have responded satisfactorily. All that's left is taste."

"Responses to strong stimuli, yes," replied Marc. "But there's a whole lot of qualitative and quantitative testing still to be done."

Leo uttered a string of "Uhhs!" drawing their attention to

his lips and an extended purple tongue flicking from left to right. He tried to lift an arm off the bed, but after only an inch or two the arm fell back down out of sheer weakness.

"It seems our patient is thirsty," acknowledged Marc. "Let him have no more than a sip or two through a straw every ten minutes. He's also quite weak, so we'll have to add nutrition to his food bag IV."

Noting Kitty's approach with two water bottles, Leo instinctively opened his mouth. From the first bottle she sprayed distilled water inside his mouth. Then she placed a straw from the second bottle between his lips. He appeared to know what to do with it and formed a suction. His eyes closed while he sipped; a simple, taste-ecstasy response relaxed his face once more.

"Muh, muh, more," they heard Leo say, as Kitty pulled away the bottle and straw.

She shook her head. "A little later." Next, she began to remove all the EEG probes and stowed them in the console drawer beneath the recorder.

Marc stuck his face directly in front of Leo's. In conversational tones, he asked, "Can you hear me? Do you have any trouble hearing me?"

Leo moved his head up and down, then back and forth incrementally like a robot. His brow wrinkled with a conflicted look, indicating that he was confused about how to answer.

"Sorry, my question is: Do you hear me all right?"

This time the delayed robotic response was a definite nod.

"Please use your voice. My name is Marc, and my colleague's name is Kitty. Do you understand what I'm saying?"

Leo's head tilted slightly while he slowly thought over the simple question. His lips parted with the muffled and trembling word "Yesss." The sound of his own voice seemed to startle him.

"Do you know your own name?" continued Marc.

Leo's dark eyes looked anxious. He desperately thought for several minutes before shaking his head and mumbling "No."

Marc said, "Your name is Leonard Tall-Chief, but everyone

calls you Leo. Does that seem familiar?"

"Nnno!" A hint of anger from frustration crept into Leo's deep, raspy voice. He sounded like he was trying to cuss, struggling against his physical weaknesses. His output was clearly unintelligible.

"Whoa! Enough! We do understand," said Marc. He spoke slowly and clearly, waiting patiently for Leo to acknowledge his words. "Most of your memory will return to you in time. You have been asleep for more than twenty years. It's called cryogenic suspension. You volunteered to be placed in a controlled coma so you could be frozen, and thus preserved, to avoid the severe effects of a terminal disease called Infirenza. The good news is that there is now a cure for Infirenza. We already administered the medication—a powerful new antibiotic—to rid you of the disease." Marc paused to let this news sink in.

"I'm…not…sick…anymore?"

Marc smiled. "No."

Leo's facial muscles relaxed, reflecting almost unbearable relief.

Marc decided it was safe to continue. "The unpleasant news is that your memory recall may take awhile. When you're feeling up to reading, we have your own autobiography, the one you submitted with your application. That may help to speed your memory recovery."

Kitty brought a pillow, fluffed it up, and tucked it under his head.

"Th…Thank you," said Leo, speaking in much clearer tones. "Whew.…Where am I?" His now thin body began to shiver. "Why is it so damn freezing in here?"

"You are in what we call a cryogenics storage farm," replied Marc. "It's like a hospital. All the sterile conditions are maintained and it's staffed by medical personnel. I'm a doctor, and Kitty here is a nurse practitioner. We keep a low ambient temperature in the lab to minimize the bacterial count. Does all that make sense to you?"

"Uh…Yeah, I think so," said Leo.

Kitty removed a backless hospital gown and blankets from a nearby cabinet shelf and helped his frail arms into the sleeves. She then covered the rest of his shivering nudity with a flannel sheet and the blankets.

"The difference is that, in this lab, we have the essential facilities to sustain the human physique under deep-freeze conditions," continued Marc. "We have an array of instruments and machinery that relieve the body's organs of their normal functions while furnishing it with all the oxygen and nutrients for its sustenance. By vacationing the organs we hope to prevent the body and its essential systems from aging. Of course, there's still a lot we don't know about that yet. You have become our longest success story so far."

"How long is that?" asked Leo.

Kitty picked up his chart and studied it long enough to make an accurate calculation. "Twenty-four years, five months and twelve days."

"Wow!" Leo looked back at Marc. "What's wrong with me? Why am I so weak?"

"There doesn't seem to be anything wrong with you that good nutrition, physical therapy, mental stimulation and exercise won't take care of."

Leo attempted to sit up. Marc extended a hand to hold his back while Kitty raised the hospital bed even higher to provide longer-term support for him. He looked around at the huge, high-ceiling room: the massive kettle resting twenty feet away, the strange machines, numerous instrument consoles, and medical paraphernalia. On his second scan, far across the room, he discovered another bed—with another patient in it!

"Who's that?" he asked, his throaty voice a mix of agitation and impatience.

"As far as we know, she is the final cryonaut remaining to be fully resuscitated from cryogenic suspension," announced Marc. "You've been sleeping alongside her for the last two decades. As soon as we move you to a private room in the special rehabilitation wing, we will attempt to revive her."

"I mean, what's her name?" persisted Leo.

"Francine Mapleton," said Kitty. "We know her simply as Fanny." She saw Leo squint, peering out to see better. "Why?" Kitty asked. "Do you recognize that name?"

"Uh…nooo," he replied in a not-so-sure voice. "I can't seem to put a face to it. Maybe it'll come to me later."

"Leo, how would you like to have that private room now?" asked Marc, as he disconnected the last of the IVs.

"Uh…Sure."

Kitty took control of the motorized bedstead. It almost had a life of its own as it rolled down a long hall to the all-chrome elevator, silently up to the third floor, down another hall, and into a corner room. The local lighting anticipated their presence and departure, turning on and off as they advanced and left each unique area.

"Open drapes," Kitty commanded to no one in particular as they entered the room. The thick purple draperies parted, letting in a glorious shining sun through a pair of tinted picture windows, overlooking a leafless pastoral scene. Although the room appeared to be largely square, the left-hand wall was considerably curved. Kitty locked the bedstead brakes and slid Leo's bony frame across to the king-sized bed.

"The room temperature and lighting work on a scale of one to ten, ten being the highest number," Kitty said, tucking him in beneath the sheet and blankets. "Simply say 'Temperature' or '"Light,' then a number in a strong, clear voice. The current plan is for you to have six meals a day, at least until you are on your feet." She looked at her wrist phone. "Your next meal is in seventy-five minutes. Physical and mental therapy are scheduled twice a day, starting tomorrow. I'll be back to check on you shortly. Meanwhile, is there anything I can get you?"

Leo's armpits dampened with sweat. He couldn't answer. Scared and confused, he dared not think about what might be in store for him in this totally new world. Still, he felt grateful to be away from the frightening cradle and sterile lab.

Kitty waited patiently, fully understanding his emotional, as well as physical, shock.

Minutes passed and he began to feel just a bit more like himself. He took a good look for the first time at this efficient woman hovering over him in starched whites. He drank in her friendly smile and even white teeth, and the small but appealing breasts on her tall, lithe body. But his thoughts shifted quickly to the woman across the room in the lab. Who was she? And they'd spent twenty-four years next to each other? Impossible to comprehend.

Chapter 10

## **Confined**
(Later that same day)

**F**ANNY'S FIRST AUDIBLE WORDS WERE: "AM I STILL sick?"

Marc and Kitty were startled by the clarity of her speech and delighted to tell her No, she was no longer sick; the miracle antibiotic had cured her of Infirenza.

The news triggered a weak but genuine smile of gratitude and relief. But her smile quickly turned fearful, and her body stiffened. "Give me a mirror, please. I need to know what I look like now. Am I horrible?"

Kitty had anticipated the request. What woman wouldn't ask? She brought a large hand mirror, and Fanny grabbed it. Within just a few seconds, her stiff anxious body relaxed.

"I look like myself...sort of," Fanny said. "My face is thinner, my shoulders and bust, too. But I can fix that. I love to eat."

"You look great, Fanny. We're proud of you," said Kitty.

In the afternoon, Fanny was transferred to a room similar to Leo's on the second floor of the same building. Almost immediately, the patient settled easily into her accommodations, eager to test all the new-fangled advancements that surrounded her. Unlike Leo's slow recall, Fanny conjured up sharp memories, particularly of her job as a waitress. Customers demanding their orders. Scolding if the "easy-over" eggs were over-fried or the coffee wasn't hot enough, even though it was the kitchen's fault. Plus the puny tips even when customers had no complaints.

In her new digs, Fanny enjoyed challenging the technology. "A glass of water, please," she said softly, not knowing how loud she needed to be. Next, hearing the sounds of ice cubes dropping, then water pouring to her right, she turned her head toward the wall in time to see a glass fill to an inch below the brim. The glass sat on a built-in shelf easily within her reach alongside a straw dispenser. *Wow!* she thought. *I could get used to this.* Feeling like a queen in her own private realm, she giggled a lot over the strange new power she now wielded over inanimate objects.

Fanny's memory continued to dredge up many other struggles, and some of the pleasant times as well, in her pre-suspended life. True, there were gaps she couldn't quite fill, but she wasn't bothered by what she didn't immediately know. But anxiety dogged her. She awoke late one night whimpering, pleading. "Mom! Mommy!" Her cries went unheard. Unstrung, forgetting the emergency button next to her bed, she lay in the dark, thrashing between the sheets, refusing to turn on the bedside light. She had a subconscious feeling that any kind of light would usher in a terrible reality. They should have cautioned her about these anxious times.

Marc and Kitty arrived at 6 a.m. and knew instinctively that this was the aspect they feared most in Fanny's recovery: crucial memories could return with calamitous results. They found her sitting up, tear-stained freckles dotting her cheeks. She wasted no time with greetings.

"Where's my mother? Have you called her to come see me?"

When Kitty took one hand in hers, Fanny jerked it away. "I want my mother!"

The ugly truth was left to Marc to explain. Shortly after Fanny left for Hybernautics, Marian Mapleton contracted Infirenza and died a few months later. She had made no effort to fight it, having lost the will to live without her daughter, her only child.

# Unto the Third Generation

Fanny grieved for days, unable or unwilling to be comforted. Although both doctor and nurse expected a reasonable period of mourning, they were alarmed by signs of Fanny's physical deterioration caused by their patient's obvious depression. Despite special shampoos proven to provide nutrients, her fluffy blonde hair had matted as if it too was depressed. Her original pre-suspension photo showed robust cheeks; now they had a pale, sunken look, markedly less healthy than expected at this stage. Marc ordered sessions with a highly regarded psychologist, but after two weeks, he saw no clear improvement.

During that time, Fanny lagged noticeably in strength and general health. She found the six daily meals stressful and annoying, picking at the food, even though the menus offered her a broad selection in advance. A matronly Nordic woman with a stern face and terse responses brought the trays each day, beginning at 7 a.m., and ending at 10 p.m. She also handled all the confined-to-bed necessities. Fanny thought of her as the Surly Viking, but knew she'd be surly too, dealing with bedpan detail. Even the state-of-the-art television with its curved, wall-size screen gave her little distraction. And reading proved even harder. Her current glasses were nearly useless. *Why aren't they giving me a new prescription?* she wondered, then grumpily realized she hadn't even let Marc know she needed one.

Another week passed. A crack appeared in Fanny's grieving demeanor and gradually widened. Kitty provided the brightest spot in her day, coming in for brief personal chats and cerebral exercises. Fanny liked the word games best, the anagrams and small crossword puzzles. The daily printout had little quizzes and provided the answers right away. Fanny was pretty good at geography, but song titles, bands and singers? Forget it. She even chuckled, realizing she had twenty-four years of catching up to do on pop culture.

Dr. Joseph Morgan came twice every day for her physical therapy—comprising reps with three-pound hand and ankle weights, stretches and sit-ups to strengthen her abs. Fanny looked forward to his visits.

"Call me Joe," he told her. This man-mountain of muscle came in a short, hairy variety with a red face and a pleasurable disposition.

Despite the tiring, relentless days, Fanny's prognosis now appeared hopeful. Her face began to take on its former roundness and her general health progressed. Even her hair woke up to its normal happy frizziness.

* * * *

**M**arc was having a tough time deflecting flack from superiors over his initiating the premature resuscitations. As a second-year resident, he had no special standing, either at the hospital or at Hybernautics. His bosses complained loudly and often about the higher cost of increased staff, extra meals, and maintenance of the high-tech rooms. Still, Marc stopped in every other day to check on his two patients' progress. He remained bold and steadfast—convinced that he was making medical history and enhancing the company's reputation. Dr. Marc thought it best that there be no connection between the two patients, so he continued to keep them a floor apart. That way he could record independent studies on each one without any cross-influences.

Immediately after her revival, Fanny had had a fleeting memory of her encounter with Leo during the recruitment training, but nary a thought of him since. Because Leo was experiencing temporary short-term memory loss, he didn't even remember inquiring about the second patient in the kettle room. The forced separation didn't concern either one of them.

* * * *

**M**ore than two weeks had passed before Leo put even one foot on the floor. Mostly, he slept and read from the wraparound video and text images projected on the TV screen. Of course, his first required reading was his autobiography. He became comfortable with his own name, and even made a few isolated associative connections with his former life. His arm strength improved enough for him to feed and groom himself. The routines paralleled Fanny's. Kitty was available part of the day to do massages, provide required mental stimulation and small talk, but he never knew when she would appear or leave. During their sessions, she exuded a mysterious warmth that puzzled him.

Joe Morgan showed up every day at ten and two for physical therapy. This time he came through the door to Leo's room holding a walker. Kitty followed him in. Leo had been waiting and sat with his long legs over the side of the bed, his swinging feet not quite touching the floor.

Leo's heart jumped a few beats. "Today?" he asked.

"Yes," Joe smiled. "Today you can try standing and maybe even take a step or two."

Joe proceeded to the center of the curved wall, tapped on it twice, and said "Open!" A hidden door popped opened a few inches. Swinging the door back revealed an adjacent room full of exercise equipment.

"Wow!" Leo burst out. "Man, this is cool."

Joe disappeared inside and reappeared a moment later with a wheelchair, which he rolled up to the bed.

The patient was heavier and stronger now with all the extra meals and therapy workouts. A fraction of his former powerful muscle tone had started to return. With Kitty holding him on one side and Joe on the other, he slid off the bed, turned slightly, and sank into the wheelchair. He'd actually stood for that single moment. Kitty pushed him into the therapy room. He was thrilled by this latest step in his recovery. He completely relaxed as she and Joe massaged and exercised his legs.

Rolling the chair up to one end of a set of parallel bars, they encouraged him to stand up once more and hold onto the bars. The first try lasted less than a minute. The second for nearly four minutes, the third for two, and the fourth was abandoned almost immediately. On the third day Leo managed three steps and learned to stand on one foot while holding onto the bars with two hands. By the end of the month he could walk the entire length of the bars, turn around, and walk all the way back, still holding on, but with only one hand. Two days later, with no hands. He'd learned to walk again. As the days went by, he graduated to the exercise machines. From then on, he walked the third floor halls at will, but was cautioned not to leave that floor—his immune system had not yet fully developed.

Leo was utterly bored with the same empty halls and the same empty rooms. His room appeared to be the only furnished one. He could spend only so many hours on the exercise machines. He was growing more and more impatient. The TV's three-dimensional movies, surround-sound music, and electronic books just weren't enough. He wanted to discover the reality of that brand-new outside world. He knew, of course, that it wasn't the same world he had left.

Leo looked forward to Kitty's visits most of all: the prescribed time scheduled for mental stimulation. He had no interest whatsoever in the word games and puzzles that appealed to Fanny. He wanted reality. In her white uniform and no makeup, Kitty felt thrilled that the patient wanted to cover new ground. She described the startling changes in the world he craved to experience. He learned all about advances in communication, vehicular power, traffic control, politics, law-making and enforcement, space travel, household inventions and conveniences, the new music and art, and even current fashion trends. But she deliberately never brought up the subject of the declining birth rate, its cause, and its world-threatening implications.

She understood that such negative news would be unwise. It might reveal her core plan, her underlying reasons for spending so much time with him. *It might drive us apart.*

Now more comfortable with each other, their chatting sometimes turned personal and each would learn a little of the other's personal life—that is, as much as Leo could bring to mind. Kitty's hazel eyes, light brown with gold flecks, looked at him tenderly under bristly lashes. She admitted to a lonely existence with no spouse and a number of failed relationships. "This job is no place to meet men," she said lightly, hoping it came off with humor. As additional weeks melted into months, their hands touched frequently. Her lips brushing his forehead or cheek seemed quite in order. They became genuine friends.

In the early days following revival, her massages were necessary to prevent bed sores. As Leo began to reacquire his former build and stature, Kitty began cutting back on their sessions. He objected, so they compromised at twice a week. During those massages, she'd lock the hall door and he'd turn up the soft rock music. He would lie naked on his stomach while she slowly rubbed in alcohol and a variety of soothing creams giving off flowery essences pleasing to the senses. A friendly slap on his rump became the cue for him to roll over and let her continue. On his backside he'd close his eyes and thoroughly enjoy the sensory transport.

Kitty stayed away from his privates, but on occasion, there would be a slight transient venture onto his forbidden parts. "Purely accidental," she assured him. Leo tried to think of it as nothing. But the power of suggestion works in mysterious ways; it rose to the occasion. He opened one eye and saw Kitty spying on him like some greedy bird of prey. He slammed his eye shut and waited for the worst. Or was it the best?

Kitty took his sudden eye action as a wink, a go-ahead. She quickly unbuttoned her blouse and unhooked her front-fastened bra, releasing her small, pert breasts. Sliding her slacks and bikini panties down, she stepped out of them and tossed them on the floor with abandon. As limber as an athlete, she mounted him. He could no more refuse her than the massages he so enjoyed. Their sudden mating was noisy, intense and deeply satisfying for both. Caution—or rather, precaution—played no part in it. When it was over, they lay side by side on the bed, short of breath and silent, shyly looking at the ceiling, each wondering whether to apologize or hunker down to seal a more permanent relationship.

"I'm sorry," he murmured. "I should have covered myself with a towel and kept decent. But no matter what, I don't want to stop feeling your magic hands and fingers."

"Thank you, you're sweet," she purred. "I know it was

highly unprofessional of me, but dear, you were so very tempting, and it's been such a long time for me."

"And you think twenty-four years isn't a long time for me?" he replied with a sheepish grin as he tidied his privates with tissues.

She rolled over onto his chest and kissed him deeply on his lips for the first time. He closed his eyes again, and enjoyed the kiss and the feel of her body against him. And then he said, "I love you, Fanny."

"What?" Kitty screamed and jerked upright. "What did you just call me?" She rolled off the bed, and snatched up her scattered clothes. Turning her back to him, she hastily pulled on her bikini panties and then her slacks as if a fire alarm had gone off.

"Kitty, wait!" he shouted. "I have no idea why I said what I did. Sweetheart, I don't even know anyone by that name. At least I don't think so."

Calmer now, facing Leo, Kitty quickly hooked her bra. "How could you have known about Fanny?" she asked as she buttoned up her blouse. "Who told you about her?"

"Kitty, I swear I don't know any Fanny." Still confused and embarrassed, Leo tried to touch her, but she moved away.

"The day we revived you," Kitty said, "there was another patient in the kettle lab. You asked Marc who she was, and he told you. The two of you had slept in the same kettle together for twenty-four years. He even told you her name." Kitty glanced in a wall mirror, ran her fingers through her short pixie cut, and smoothed her bangs.

Leo protested. "But how could I remember her name when I don't have all my short-term memory back yet? I'm still not so sure about my own name."

"Could you have had a relationship before instillation?" Kitty asked. "An old flame maybe? Somebody you cared about?"

"I don't think so," he said, racking his brain for answers. "Maybe if I met the woman I might remember her. Is she still here? In the building, I mean."

"Uh…yesss," Kitty said, wondering why she answered at all.

"Is that why I'm confined to the third floor?" he asked.

Her eyes rolled. This time she didn't answer at all.

Leo's chiseled face with its high cheekbones turned stormy. "I have no particular reason for wanting to meet this Fanny person. But if there's some meaningful justification for your keeping us apart, I want to know what it is. What's going on here, Kitty? Is this your doing?"

"No! I had nothing to do with it," she sputtered. "It's company policy. Something to do with keeping projects separate and not letting them affect or influence each other. I sure don't think they'd approve of what just happened here either."

"I'd bet on it," said Leo. His wide mouth turned into a mischievous grin. "But that doesn't mean we can't make our own policy, does it? I want us to continue. Don't you?" He held his arms out to her. His eyes pleaded with hers.

She hesitated, but only for a moment, then rushed at him, allowing him to envelop her completely. *No way I'm going to let him meet Fanny, not if I can help it.* After a minute she looked up in his face and kissed him long and hard. "I've got to get back now or Marc will come looking for me." She wiggled out of his embrace. He tried to slip his strong arms around her once more, but she escaped quickly into the hall and disappeared.

Chapter 11

# Rejection
(The year 2085)

NINE WEEKS LATER, LEO HAD FILLED OUT TO HIS pre-Infirenza self: healthy and robust, with sinewy neck, defined biceps and forearms, powerful chest and thigh muscles. He felt somewhat satisfied; yet real peace eluded him. There was no reason for him to be agitated. The accommodations, meals, and entertainment fare were more than adequate. In a sardonic way he thought of Marc and Kitty as his handlers. Kitty monitored his vital statistics daily. His hospital gowns had been replaced with khakis and polo shirts. Marc showed him medical reports that trumpeted Hybernautics' brilliant cryogenic success.

Leo and Kitty managed a frisky tussle in bed at least twice weekly. He told her he loved her, but his words sounded hollow even to himself. It wasn't that bell-ringing, struck-by-lightning love affair he'd always imagined and yearned for as a single guy in his early twenties. He couldn't figure out the wrong of it. The sex worked just fine. Kitty was more than obliging. He couldn't imagine her being more attentive or caring. But her professional duties elsewhere left him to himself for the better part of most days.

Fragments of his long-term memory had returned, reminding him that he'd had a  profession of his own. Being a high-steel man was never just a job, dangerous as it was, but work of value to his city, with tangible results and paycheck rewards: buildings he and his coworkers could be proud of. What was he now at forty-seven?

Leo became lonely, almost needy, and boredom reigned. He prowled the halls, the inner perimeter of the building. The mere sight of the great outdoors through the giant picture windows exhilarated him. The greening of springtime, fresh with budding trees and sprouting flowers, spelled hope and fed his curiosity. What next? The skimpy window locks, the broad elevator entrance, and the fire stairs reminded him that he needn't be a prisoner in these upper halls. Leo believed he could simply walk away any time he so pleased. The only bond that kept him in check was the fragile, yet seemingly essential one he'd forged with Kitty. He wanted to explore the changed world, but was it worth giving up what he had here? He knew he'd have to leave at some point. But when? What did they have in store for him, if anything? Was he now just an exotic, expensive lab-rat experiment?

There was another itch Leo couldn't scratch. *Who is this Fanny I shared a kettle with for twenty-four years? And why did I blurt out her name at the most inopportune time and place? Or wasn't it her name? Was I married or pledged to another Fanny in my former life? Not according to my autobiography. I wish I could recall more of the truth. And why is Kitty so skittish when I mention this Fanny's name or ask about her? After all, we had the same harrowing experiences: disease and time-suspension. It couldn't do any harm to talk about it with her sometime.*

Around ten o'clock one Tuesday night Leo was sprawled out in his recliner reading Ray Bradbury's *The Martian Chronicles*, when Kitty showed up—out of her severe white uniform, in a flowered mini-dress that showed off her slender, supple legs. Surprised, he tossed the paperback on the end table and stood to greet her. They came together in a silent embrace, kissed briefly, and she began to disrobe nonchalantly when Leo sprang his startling questions.

"Why are we always meeting on the sly in my room? What

are we ashamed of? If we're in love, why can't we shout it from the rooftops? What's wrong with that?"

Kitty stood motionless for a minute or two in pink lace bra and matching bikini panties, as she matter-of-factly folded her dress. She said absolutely nothing.

"What's wrong with that?" Leo repeated. "Why can't we have sex at your place—in your bedroom, in your bed some-times?"

Kitty tried to compose a credible response. "This is a place of business. After all, I have to maintain a degree of professional-ism among my colleagues."

His dark eyes flashed. "Oh, bullshit! I've barely seen a half-dozen people the whole time I've been here, and none of them look like they even give a damn how you and I behave. You don't even have an on-site supervisor. So what gives? Are you jealous of Fanny, someone I don't even remember? Or are you merely ashamed to be with me? Are you here for just the sex? Huh?"

Without saying a word, Kitty unfolded her dress, slid it over her head, and wriggled her arms into it. As she adjusted the fabric around her hips and into place, their eyes met—his inquir-ing, hers cold and hard. Not all of her reluctance to continue could be attributed to his accusations. More of it might be credited to her feeling of guilt: the realization that Leo might just be right. *Is sex so important to me? What were my real motives for seducing him? Was the purpose of it so obvious? Am I so intent on having a child that I've ignored both our feelings, ignoring love altogether?* Angry at her-self, she pivoted and started to leave.

"Wait!" Leo cried, when he realized that she intended to walk out on him.

An over-the-shoulder frigid stare was all he got in return as Kitty headed out the door and down the hall to the elevator.

* * * *

**T**hree weeks had passed since Leo and Kitty had locked horns. She had stopped coming to his room altogether. Joe's physi-cal therapy sessions had long since ceased; Leo didn't need them any more. The only person he now encountered was Kim Su'u, the small, bent Asian man who brought his meals—now down from six to four per day to slow down his weight gain. But Kim spoke only in nods and polite bows. Leo wasn't sure whether the slight, pale man didn't want to engage in conversation or didn't speak English. Nevertheless, Leo stopped trying to pry words from him.

One morning as he prowled the halls, he encountered a woman just exiting the elevator: Kitty! Both were stunned by the unexpected meeting and behaved like mere acquaintances. Their bland exchange never left the usual weather and health platitudes until suddenly, in a fit of pent-up anger, Kitty blurted out, "I'm three months pregnant—with your child!"

Leo stood rock-still, his mouth agape, a flush rising from his neck to his high forehead. Why was he so surprised? They had never taken any precautions. His prolonged silence so infuriated her that she quickly returned to the elevator and ordered the doors shut. She never heard him shout, "Wait! Don't go!"

Despite Leo's efforts to recall the elevator, that intelligent conveyance didn't respond for five minutes. He had never been allowed in it. When the doors finally spread open, he discovered the lack of visible controls. He'd heard others using voice commands, but there was more to it: voice recognition. Not everyone could captain its motion. He tried a few commands, but when they failed, he ran to a picture window in time to see a strange hovering vehicle leave the parking facility and swiftly disappear down a tree-lined passage. Where were all the cars? The vehicle was nothing like a clumsy, ear-splitting helicopter. This contraption was shaped like an oval giant insect with a dome-like transparent roof and small but powerful rotors. *Man, I've gotta get myself one of those.*

* * * *

**F**rustrated and furious, he frequently tried to contact Kitty, but pushing the call button in his room produced only the ever-silent Kim. Leo took the stairs, but they led only to fire doors on the first and second floors. There were no phones, neither cell nor landline available for his use. After all, who would he call after two decades sealed off from the civilized world?

Days passed. His hope for Kitty's eventual return diminished. His reasons for staying in Hybernautics' care eroded with it. More and more, his thoughts turned to the outside world. *It's easy,* he tried to assure himself. *I can just walk through those double doors and down the stairs and out onto the street. But it's not the same world I knew. Are there things I should know before I blunder out of here? No one has said I can't go. But what will I do out there? I have no money. Do they still use dollars? Or some other new, strange currency? And what if I can't handle it and want to come back here? Will they let me back in?*

The next day Kim did not bring his breakfast. A smiling Dr. Marc Litton entered the room pushing his food cart. Leo expected him to leave the food and depart immediately, but Marc seemed amenable to both remaining and chatting while Leo ate. He explained that he brought the food because Kim had broken his arm falling down in the kitchen. The doctor's sharp features and narrow chin shifted into a contrite expression. "Sorry I haven't been more attentive to you, Leo. I'm in my last year of residency now and the hospital has offered me a full-time position as a cardiac surgeon. It's a big step for me. I'm glad to see you doing so well—Joe's reports on your physical therapy results are excellent. I'm here today for your routine physical."

Just as Marc reached for his medical case, Leo bluntly asked, "How's Kitty Fairchild doing?"

Marc peered at him through rimless spectacles. "I'm sorry to inform you of unpleasant news. Kitty is having a rough time. She took maternity leave a little over a month ago. She was hospitalized just last week, so I called her there. She miscarried."

"Oh, no!" gasped Leo.

"Terrible news, but I understand she's recuperating physically. Emotionally, she's grieving, which is to be expected."

"I'm so sorry. I'd like to tell her that myself. Even better, I want to visit her."

"You are the father, aren't you?" asked Marc.

Leo's rugged face colored. "Yes, of course, but we had this awful misunderstanding and never had the opportunity to resolve it. I think I do love her."

Marc's forehead turned into a deep frown. "You think you love her! Don't you even know?"

"How can I be sure? I've never loved anyone before. At least let me go and see her."

"More bad news, Leo. Kitty didn't name you specifically, but she told me she didn't want anything to do with the father of her baby. I have to respect that."

"Damn it, why?" Leo asked. "Doesn't she love me?"

"She didn't say why. I wasn't even supposed to tell you, but you seemed so concerned."

"What happened to the baby? We were a healthy couple, at least I thought so. Was it me? Something to do with Infirenza? Or maybe the cryogenic suspension?"

Marc hesitated. "Yes and no."

"What the hell kind of cockamamie answer is that?" Leo blurted out.

Marc had never heard the word "cockamamie" before, but got the sense of it and certainly understood his patient's panic. "Leo, it's complicated. First of all, Kitty selected you for a lover because, in her world, you were the ideal donor, the only available donor, in fact. It was obvious she wanted a baby, your baby, if possible."

"I don't understand," said Leo, angry now. "That's hard to believe. With her good looks, her upbeat personality, her excellent job—a woman like her could have anyone she wanted. Why zero in on me? Why my baby?"

"It's a very long story, Leo," Mark said, "so please take a deep breath, sit down in your recliner…That's it, and let me explain. While you were in cryogenic suspension awaiting a cure for Infirenza, the rest of world was feasting on a brand-new array of delicious and supposedly healthy synthetic foods called Synthom-anna. It controlled body weight and provided relief from many allergies. Besides, it came so cheap in so many tasty forms that its use spread across most economic and geographic boundaries worldwide. Before long, just about everyone alive consumed it."

"For crissake, what's food got to do with all this?" interrupted Leo.

"Everything," replied Marc.

"I do remember hearing something about the synthetic food craze. I suppose that fad is long gone by now."

"Unfortunately no, not by a long shot," said Marc. "The scientific community didn't understand the long-term, widespread effects of Synthomanna soon enough. By the start of the third generation, it was discovered that people weren't having babies, and the world population was rapidly declining. You, my dear boy, and a small, scattered population of others, were spared. Kitty was keenly aware of that. She believed the fault lay with the males of the human species, and she had learned that no amount of erection enhancement could make a difference. In her mind, the two of you could produce a healthy baby."

"It sounds plausible. So what went wrong?"

"Her one-sex premise was faulty. Both the male and female populations were susceptible to the effects of this synthetic food product. A whole raft of scientific studies supports this conclusion. The few women who actually achieved conception miscarried in either the fourth or fifth month. Kitty was merely another statistic of this tragic outcome—and so was your child."

"Jeez!" exclaimed Leo. "And there's no counter or reversal drug to combat these miscarriages?"

"Nope, but they're working twenty-four-seven on it," said Marc. "You are still capable of reproduction. At least, you have a strong sperm count. The fetus bore that out as well. That's why we've taken such good care of you."

"Does this mean I'm the last virile man on earth?"

"Hardly, but certainly one of the very few. Quite an enviable status, I might add." A broad smile escaped from Marc.

"Enviable, maybe, but what good is it when there's no one

to appreciate it?"

"No one?" repeated Marc. "I think you're misinformed."

"Ah, the waiting mystery woman, the lady downstairs. What about Fanny?" asked Leo. "Can she deliver the goods properly?"

"As far as we know, she can. But how the hell do you know about Fanny?" asked Marc.

"I must have known her from my life before suspension. I just don't remember anything about her. Somehow her name slipped out the first time Kitty and I had sex. It was a goddamn bad moment. She got all upset. I finally convinced her I had no idea why I said Fanny's name and got her to explain who Fanny was. The name came up on another occasion when I suggested we announce our love to the world. In fact, that's when she ran out on me. Kitty actually sounded jealous."

"That's too bad. Now let's see how you're progressing." Marc spent the next hour taking vital signs and examining Leo's entire body with digital scanning and recording devices. The recordings would be analyzed, along with blood, urine and semen samples. When he finished, he said, "As I thought, you're in excellent health, allowing for the slightly raised heart rate due to all the shocking news I've brought you. Do you have any further questions for me?"

"Yeah. Is there any reason why I can't just walk out of here? Am I some kind of prisoner now that you guys have re-created the whole me? Am I merely a patient with expectations of an eventual discharge, or have I become a guinea pig to be experimented on—a trained monkey to perform on demand?"

Marc spoke in a reassuring voice. "I understand exactly how you feel. You're free to go any time you wish, although we *would* like to do a number of experiments with you as the reproductive so-called chief stud. Are you willing?"

"With this Fanny from downstairs?" asked Leo. He made a screwed-up distasteful face.

"By any man's standards she's quite pretty, but right now she's the only viable mate. You'll get a chance to meet her, check her out, and then it'll be up to you."

Leo scowled. "Not very romantic, is it? Sounds a bit too scientific for me. I'll have to think it over some."

Leo mulled it over for several days. *I'm not so hard up for sex that I have to perform on demand under some weird scientific conditions.* He knew that even if his efforts didn't result in babies, there was a whole world of willing women out there for him to sample. But curiosity got the better of him. *I'll just have to see this Fanny babe first. Then I'll decide.*

Chapter 12

# Restraint

**L**EO TRIED WEIGHING THE STARK OPTIONS DR. Marc Litton had laid on him. *Am I taking too much time to decide? I'm not the only cryonaut on the block. One or more of the others could be the hero and save the doomed human race from its present dire straits. And what the hell do I owe science and the rest of mankind, anyway? On the other hand, what if this Fanny is the only female cryonaut able to have children? Wouldn't I have the honor of being remembered as the second father of the human race—my personal ticket to immortality? But what if Fanny turns out to be ugly, fat and repulsive?* Even so, Leo couldn't let go of the guilt that he was somehow shirking a moral responsibility. It tugged at him like an unrelenting dog tearing at his pants cuff.

He was acutely aware that Hybernautics had not given him celebrity status after his distillation and recovery. The local news media had carried a few items on his progress, fed to it as press releases from the company. But he'd expected to be greeted with fanfare: TV interviews and speaking invitations, like the returning astronauts had been thirty, forty years ago. It hadn't happened. *Does Hybernautics ever plan to? And do I really want them to?* Leo's tweaked memory reminded him that some astronauts didn't fare so well. John Glenn had remained a hero and emotionally stable, but some others ended up as alcoholics, divorced, or even let go from the program.

All in all, his personal freedom spoke louder than duty, so when he was good and ready to leave, he shook his pillow out of its case and began to pack shaving and grooming articles, plus a few changes of clothes. Stealing? No! They owed him at least this much. When he finished packing, he headed out into the hall and over to the double-door exit. He pushed down on the release bar and went through one of the doors to the fire stairs and started down. At the second floor landing another set of double doors stared back at him. What intrigued him most was that a wooden wedge held one of those doors wide open, leading into the corridor. He needed to take only one more flight downstairs. He knew it led outside and to freedom.

But Leo couldn't move, as though a powerful magnet was drawing him toward the second-floor space. At first, he suspected that Marc had set a trap for him, but then another, stronger, force took a firm hold of him. *What is this Fanny like? What will I be missing? Will there really be other choices in my future?* Curiosity gripped him and led him down the hall. He stared into the rooms one by one. Each one was deserted, until he came to the one that wasn't.

Stunned, Leo stood for a moment in the door frame, admiring a plumpish female silhouette standing a few feet away. Finally, "Hello, are you Fanny?"

"Oh!" she shrieked and spun around to face him. "You startled me. I didn't know anyone was standing there. Yes, that's my name. Who are you? Wait! Haven't we met before?"

"My name is Leonard Tall-Chief, but everyone calls me Leo. Apparently, we met before as kettle mates."

"Kettle mates?" she returned with a quizzical expression.

"Yeah, kettle mates. I don't think we were actually introduced, but we slept next to each other for twenty-four years in that contraption."

"Ah, the kettle," she said with a coy smile. "That's not exactly like sleeping together, is it now? I do have a maiden's reputation to consider."

"I assure you your reputation is still intact, but I can't guarantee it will remain so under this roof. The evil ones in charge here have other ideas. I, on the other hand, pretend to be honorable."

"Ooh, that sounds ominous," she declared, her round cheeks breaking into deep dimples. "Tall-Chief, that sounds like you're a Native American."

"My paternal great-grandfather was a proud, full-blooded Iroquois. He married outside the Iroquois nation. My great-grandmother was a Cayute. My grandfather married a Caucasian, and so on, leaving me with only a smidgen of Indian heritage. I do value who I am, though."

"Where have you been since distillation and resuscitation?"

"Upstairs on the third floor. But for some unknown reason I called out your name when I least expected to. I'm having trouble remembering things that happened just prior to instillation."

Her blonde eyebrows arched in surprise. "Sorry about your memory. I've gotten past all my memory problems now. I recall everything quite clearly."

"But did we know each other?" he persisted.

"We did meet for a few minutes during recruiting. We sat next to each other in the waiting room. We exchanged names and talked some." She looked down at his pillowcase. "What's in the sack, Leo?"

"Uh, a few things for my trip. I'm leaving the facility. I've had enough of confinement. I want to get out and see this new world."

"You're leaving?" Disappointment bore down on the corners of her full lips. She looked away.

"Then it *was* a conspiracy," he declared.

"Conspiracy?" she questioned.

"Yeah! You were expecting me, weren't you?"

"Yes," she murmured.

"You were briefed on everything, too?"

"Yes."

"The open door was a welcome mat! You and the good doctor laid a trap for me. So much for your so-called honor. You intended to use me all along, didn't you?"

Her green eyes glinted with humor. "Of course."

"Why?"

"Isn't it obvious? I don't want to go through life without experiencing motherhood. I was born for that role. I was a waitress in a diner just to pay the bills. But I want something more out of life. Besides I was kind of attracted to you when we met during recruitment. As a matter of fact, I still am, and I noticed you paid me a little attention, too."

He reddened. "I did?" Looking down at her, almost a head shorter, he thought, *I can see why.* He liked the untamed blonde mop, the fullness of her upper arms in a sleeveless dress, the curved bottom he'd noticed when he first approached her room. *I like the way she moves and talks. I could do a lot worse.*

"Yep!" she replied, in a clipped, chirpy voice. "If I may make a suggestion, why don't you give it a try? In the meantime you could move into one of the empty rooms on either side of mine. Let's take our time and get better acquainted. At best, we can enjoy some much-needed companionship. Maybe nature will be kind and accomplish the rest."

"Companionship?" repeated Leo. "I thought Marc's objective was laboratory-sterile copulation. You know: wham-bam, thank you, ma'am. I didn't know he had any long-term plans for us."

"I don't know what heroic propaganda Marc has been filling your head with, but I, personally, don't want to miss out on the possibility to pursue genuine love and a normal family life. Call it an old-fashioned courtship, if you will, but it's what I want. In fact, I insist on it. The goal, of course, is for us to breed, regardless of our ultimate relationship."

"What happens if we're not a match?" he asked, scratching the back of his neck. "What if, after all that, we find we're not compatible husband and wife prospects?"

"I will still make my body available to you as promised. The very worst that can happen is *you* decide not to mate and hit the proverbial road, as you intended a few minutes ago. What can you lose?"

"A simple bedding down! No commitments?" His thoughts momentarily buzzed about like a persistent mosquito, recollecting the unloved baby he'd just lost; a tinge of regret suffusing his tense body. "Not even if there's a child involved?"

"I want a child no matter what," she replied. "However, there's always the danger that I'll develop sincere, strong feelings for you, and you might not feel the same way about me. I'm willing to take the risk. I kind of like you already. Of course, if you ever get the ideas of husband and fatherhood set firmly between your ears, along with an overwhelming sense of love for me and the family we might produce, I'd say we'll have something well worth pursuing—that is, marriage. Otherwise, you'll be free to deposit your seed and leave. What do you say to that?"

Her speech made him dizzy. She sounded like a professor prepping students for an exam. But still, he was intrigued. "I say it sounds non-threatening. What's the catch?" Leo scanned her full image once more and felt a stirring inside him. *Not only is she a lot prettier than Kitty, she's more buxom and certainly a good deal more honest.*

"I assure you there is no catch." *Damn*, she thought, *he's quite a hunk. Why am I trying so hard to convince him not to jump into my panties when that's exactly what I want most? Well maybe not most—I do want the rest.*

"Yeah, I'm interested. When do I move in?" He dropped his pillowcase bundle on her bed.

Now it was Fanny's turn to blush. "No time like the present. Let's get you settled next door. But first…" She pushed past him and a few steps down the hall to a linen closet, where she popped open the doors and laid a pile of bedding on his outstretched arms. "Follow me," she said. *Funny*, she thought, *I spent my working life taking orders from others, and now I'm the one issuing orders. Maybe I'd better cool it.* She led the way into the room next to hers.

"Are separate accommodations necessary?" he asked.

"Not if you're bent on a one-night stand. Actually, I was hoping for more than that—some romancing, a wooing of sorts, maybe friendship first. Every woman wants to know what the father of her children will be like. But the choice is yours, Leo. All yours."

"You're looking for foreplay, maybe?" he asked, grinning sheepishly as he laid the linens down on a chair.

Fanny took one end of the sheet from the pile and together they stretched it across the bed. "You're joking, of course."

"Sure, Fanny. I think I understand where you're coming from. I can wait." What he really wanted was to reach out and gather her to him. *I wonder what her lips taste like. I wonder what her body would feel like next to mine.* He groaned aloud with pleasure.

Fanny suddenly looked up from securing the fitted sheet and saw his expression. She quickly reacted by folding her arms across her chest. "You're undressing me in your mind, aren't you?"

"Sorry, I can't help it. I find you very, very attractive."

"Is that what you do with every girl you meet?"

"No, of course not. I...I haven't dated that much. But what's with the third degree?"

Fanny ignored the question and pursued her obsession.

"You're not telling me you're still a virgin, are you?"

"Oh, no, nothing like that." He bit his lip when thoughts of Kitty flashed through his mind.

"Good," she said, "I don't like lying. I know you had a thing going with Kitty. Got her pregnant, too." Fanny finished spreading a lightweight blanket at the foot of the bed.

"Yeah. You know a lot about me, probably more than I know about myself. But Kitty's done with me and I'm done with her. It's all kaput now."

"I know. Marc told me all about it. Sorry about the baby."

She slipped the pillow into its case, plumped it up, and propped it at the head of the bed.

"Thank you, but it's probably for the best. I felt bad for Kitty. As it turned out, we weren't that compatible. She had her own agenda, and it didn't include me in the long run. I became expendable."

Fanny strolled around the bed to his side, stood on tiptoe, and bussed him quickly on the cheek before he knew what was happening. He tried to slip his arms around her, but she was away in a flash, into her own room.

He scampered after her. "Wait up. Is that all for today? Is our friendship going to be rationed?"

"Rationed?" she questioned. "What do you mean?"

"Are we done for the day? Do I have to keep chasing you to keep the conversation going?" Leo asked.

"No, of course not. We have separate rooms to afford each of us a measure of personal privacy when we want or need it. However, our doors are never locked, so if you come to my room or I to yours, it's because we want to be together. I scooted away after that kiss because I wanted to avoid any premature intimacy. We can't just jump into bed and call it quits, can we? We'd never know if there's that something special in store for us. Even you might regret having closed that door too quickly."

Leo felt a tug of doubt. *Is she always so bossy?* Her tone sounded like he was being lectured—back in fifth grade in the principal's office for clowning around. Grudgingly, he said, "I suppose I can handle separate rooms, as long as you're next door. So where do we go from here?"

Fanny sensed the hesitation and softened. She reached out, took both of his hands in her own, and squeezed gently, then let go.

"Take a walk with me?"

"Of course, dear." She linked her arm in his, and they headed down the hall. The two enormous windows revealed a gray, rain-soaked panorama of manicured lawns and shrubs, a blacktop lot with a few scattered hovercraft in its spaces, and a forested park beyond.

"Makes you glad you're inside all warm and dry and fuzzy, doesn't it?" offered Fanny.

He frowned and ran his fingers through his thick black hair. "Not really. There's a powerful mystique about being on the other side of that glass—outside, unbound, and free to go anywhere you please. There's a whole world out there waiting to be explored."

"Oh, Leo, I didn't realize you haven't been outside these walls yet."

"And you have, Fanny?"

"A few times, but never alone and never that far from home," she said.

"Damn it, Fanny! Where the hell are we? And that road down there, where does it go?"

"We're somewhere in upper Minnesota. Didn't Marc or Kitty tell you? I don't drive one of those contraptions, and town is just too far to walk. No one has offered to drive me either."

"Pucevale is the name of the facility," he said, reading the sign on the lawn. "Could it be the town's name as well?"

"I'm afraid I don't know that either," she replied. "I suppose we could ask Marc."

Leo took hold of Fanny's hand, and the two strolled the second-floor perimeter twice. As they approached the open door of Leo's room, they discovered a small table set with two chairs and two prepackaged, preheated dinners. Chewy chicken, peas, mashed potatoes, and cherry pie. Leo dutifully gobbled it all up and set his fork down with a clatter. "Know what? This stuff is crap. I'm sick of it. I wanna go to a restaurant and get barbecued ribs or chili or a T-bone steak."

"Me too," she mumbled, swallowing a large mouthful. "I never liked chicken breast, it's always dry. But you know what else?" She cocked her head, and with eyes bright said, "Leo, your memory's coming back. Mine is too. I miss veal parmesan and Chinese. But at least we're lucky we didn't get stuck eating the so-called miracle food. Apparently, when we were in the kettles it was targeted at first to the Third World."

"Yeah, that's true," he said. "There must be something better to eat on the outside. Do they have restaurants in this burg? Pucevale. What an ugly name. Sounds like Pukevale."

Fanny erupted in a torrent of giggles—the first time Leo had heard her laugh.

They retired to the couch to watch movies on the wall vision set. The trays were removed sometime during the evening without them ever noticing.

Midway through the second film, Leo fell asleep, and his large head naturally slouched down to rest on Fanny's shoulder. At first she enjoyed the pleasant closeness and the smell of his aftershave. But her shoulder soon felt sore, and he started making random sleep noises, even an occasional snore. Disengaging herself, she substituted a sofa bolster for her shoulder and returned to her own room for the night.

Two hours later Leo awoke—disappointed. Nature was calling, the bathroom beckoned. He'd been dreaming of corn on the cob, a huge plateful, and he hadn't even gotten to take one bite.

Chapter 13

## More Doubts

The next morning the easterly sun burst
through the broad opening in the drapes, jolting Leo awake. His
head sank back into the pillow in a pleasant haze, Lying motionless
on his back, he lazily contemplated the events of the previous day.
A sweet image seized possession of his thoughts. *Ah, the delectable
Fanny. Am I falling helplessly? Is she mesmerizing me into her life? Has
she gotten me to commit to more than I bargained for? Damn, she's
beautiful.*

Jumbled voices dissolved the fantasy. They were coming
from the next room, and he knew whose they were. Tossing the
covers back, he swung his brawny legs over the edge of the bed
and reached for his khakis. One foot, the other, an upward tug and
then a belting at the waist. Pulling on a T-shirt, he raced to the
bathroom to brush his teeth. Trying to slap his wild hair into place,
he padded barefoot out into the hall and next door.

Fanny and Marc were sitting at the table next to the window eating breakfast. Coming closer, Leo saw there were three
trays there—one for him as well.

"Ah, sleeping beauty arrives," said Marc.

"Beard and all," said Fanny, wrinkling her upturned small
nose.

Leo's fingers scraped his cheek. He shrugged and turned

to leave.

"Wait!" cried Marc. "Don't go!"

"Stay!" said Fanny. "Your breakfast will get cold. I've seen unshaven faces before. Besides, Marc has brought us some news."

"Good or bad?" Leo asked, striding back to the table with renewed energy.

"Mixed, I'm afraid," said Marc. "I got a letter yesterday ordering the permanent closing of this facility. As of next Friday, the two of you are without a place to live. Now that my residency is over, I'll be starting my full-time job at the hospital. Frankly, I'll miss the two of you. Very much."

Leo wasn't listening to the last part. Dropping into his chair, he said, "Wow, only nine days! Is there anything in the letter for us low-life cryonauts?"

"As a matter of fact, there is, and that's the good news. Each of you will receive a stipend of $50,000 in cash to start a new life—another $20,000 per child if your matings result in offspring. There are a few other fine points you'll have to read for yourself: education, health care, mostly affecting the assumed children."

A tiny tear rolled down Fanny's right cheek. "Nothing like applying pressure from the get-go."

"Hey, are you that much in love with this place?" Marc tried to make light of their dire situation as he plucked a tissue from the table dispenser and handed it to her.

"It's not that, Marc, it's the shock. We have to find a place to stay, and I haven't the faintest idea of how to go about it." Fanny wiped away the lone tear and dabbed at the corners of both eyes.

Marc tried to sound reassuring. "I could run the two of you into town after breakfast and pick you up later, maybe around five. There's a realtor on Main Street. Maybe she can set you two on the right path."

"Suppose we don't want to settle in Minnesota?" said Leo, picking up a strip of bacon. Maybe we'd like someplace warmer. We haven't talked about it yet."

"If that's what you both want," Marc said. "Then I suggest

you pack up your few belongings, and I'll whisk you off to the bank to cash your checks, and then to the bus stop to choose your city of destination. I'll hate to see you go." He tried to joke. "I was just beginning to get used to the likes of you."

Fanny squirmed in her chair and tried to control her panicked voice. "Let's not be too hasty here. I'd like to have a look at this little burg down the road first. Can we put off the bus thing for a day or two?"

The doctor paused, then measured his words. "Sure, anything you two agree on." His eyes darted from one to the other, knowing the lid was about to blow.

"Suppose we can't agree? What then?" Leo asked.

Fanny's chubby jaw dropped. "What?" she blurted in disbelief. "You bastard!"

Leo blinked, his wide forehead cleaving into a scowl. "Keep your shirt on, woman. It's only a what-if question." He took a long slurp of coffee, wondering who this suddenly hotheaded babe was sitting across from him.

Marc quickly intervened. "The answer is that I would then be pleased to accommodate each of you individually. However, I must warn you that there's a flip side to the company's generosity. If you choose to go your separate ways without mating, your stipend gets reduced by half."

"Who's making the rules and footing the bill on this?" asked Leo, chomping his way through another strip of bacon.

"I don't know for sure," replied Marc. "The letterhead is Hybernautics. The letter is signed by the CEO, Dr. Horace Richards, but it could be the dictate of some Federal Government grant. Let's face it, though, it's a sizeable amount of money to have gotten past the company's stockholders."

Leo wiped his lips with a paper napkin and looked over at Fanny. "This deadline speeds things up. Your get-acquainted plan doesn't account for so little time."

"You can wipe that smirk off your face, Mr. Tall-Chief," snapped Fanny. "I hear you. I can see you've already made up your mind to drop your seed and bolt. I give up. Okay, tonight's the night at eight. No preliminaries, just the no-commitments mating you've always wanted. I hope you're satisfied, Mr. Tall-Chief." Her whole body, in shocking-pink blouse and matching pants, actually trembled.

"Whoa!" responded Leo. "I've accepted your terms and I've even warmed to your charms."

"You have?"

"Yeah! So where the hell is all this anger coming from?" he asked.

"I thought maybe you had changed your mind," Fanny said, a slight whimper in her voice. "You seemed so totally pleased that our bonding time would be shortened."

He shook his head. "I don't know what I have to do to convince you that I'm committed to you and your plan. Sure, I'll have a look at the burg down the road here. It's just that I'm a planner and when I look to the future, I want to see a pleasant climate, a good job, and some compatible neighbors. I'm a skilled, high-steel worker. I don't see the likelihood of many tall buildings in a tiny town. Besides, I've nothing against the neighbors, but Minnesota has some wicked winters. Probably worse than Columbus. But I'm game, so bring it on, Fanny girl."

A subdued Fanny turned to the doctor. "Marc, I'd like to take you up on your offer to drive us to town and pick us up later."

Marc looked over at Leo, who nodded his okay. "Sure thing, Fanny. Meet me downstairs in an hour. You can spend the whole day there and give me a call when you're ready to return for the night."

Leo shoved the remainder of his scrambled egg onto the last slice of toast, folded it in half, and took a huge bite. Swallowing the last mouthful, he rose to his bare feet. "See you in an hour," he said, and padded back to his room.

"Yes," Fanny replied.

Anxious thoughts rattled around in Leo's head. *We're going to be out in the cold. So little warning. Getting kicked out with no counseling, not even a goddamned map of the United States! My whole future—our future, if we have one—is up in the air.*

Chapter 14

## Panic in the Park

THEIR FLEET MAYFLOWER HOVERMOBILE SPED toward the town of Pucevale down the tree-lined lane eight feet aloft. On this lovely May day in the 70s, Fanny and Leo wore shorts for the first time in over twenty years. Fanny rode up front with Marc, leaving Leo with plenty of leg room in the rear seat. Inside, the high-pitched whine could hardly be heard. Outside, the green countryside danced by. The clear-glass bubbletop allowed them a perfect view, except that the vehicle moved with such speed it almost blurred their vision.

"Hey, Doc, could you slow down? This is my first venture into the new world. What's the big rush?" Leo asked.

"Sorry," Marc said. "Confession time. I've always been a wannabe race driver." He slowed, then hovered above one of three traffic lights in the small town. The light changed from red to green and Marc turned onto Main Street, halted halfway down the block, and settled them at the curb in front of the Pucevale National Bank. To Leo and Fanny the landing felt more like a high-speed elevator out of control. Their stomachs flipped back into place.

"Welcome to Pucevale in all its glory," Marc said, releasing the bubbletop. It slowly rose to a 45-degree angle. Leo had to duck to climb out. Marc handed Fanny a smart phone. "Here's my iTalk-85, it's the newest version. Call me when you want to return. My number is preprogrammed at the top of the list. Oh, by the way, there's a lovely little park in the next block."

"Thanks," she said. She couldn't wait to scroll through and try all the apps. She'd never been able to afford any kind of cell phone.

Inside the bank they sat down and waited for service at the new accounts desk. Beverly Carroll, the assistant bank manager, called them into her office. "How can I help you?"

"We would like to open two accounts, one for each of us, and make some rather large deposits," said Leo.

"How large would that be? Our current policy is to withhold all but $200 for seventy-two hours. Will that be satisfactory?"

"I guess so," said Leo. "The deposits will be $50,000 each." They displayed their Hybernautics checks.

"Supposing I start with the young lady. Name?"

Thus began a question and answer exchange that lasted an hour, with two full pages entered into the computer. Beverly completed Fanny's paperwork, then followed with Leo's. It all went smoothly until two important entries: their birth dates. The elderly banker squinted, nervously smoothed her already-tidy gray hair, and lapsed into puzzled silence. They both looked too young to be in their forties.

Leo decided to jump in before the whole deal collapsed. "Ms. Beverly," he said in a gentle voice, "let me explain. Fanny and I work for Hybernautics. We were the company's last two cryonauts—in suspended animation for twenty-four years."

"My goodness!" fluttered Beverly. "How silly of me not to recall. I did follow your adventures in our local news. I must say, it's a pleasure to meet you both. You were very brave—I can't even imagine—and quite the celebrities, in my mind, anyway." She handed them account identification cards and credit cards. Because they had no permanent addresses, they agreed to automatic credit-card billing, charged against their bank accounts. Beverly vigorously shook their hands and, glowing with importance, wished them much luck and success.

As they emerged back out on the street, Fanny giggled. "I bet she couldn't wait for us to leave so she could tell her coworkers about us."

Leo grinned. "Yeah. Nice lady. But somehow I expected the whole process to be faster, more automated. Two decades, they're still doing some stuff the same old way."

Not so in the convenience store a few doors down the block. No clerks. All self-checkout, but surveillance cameras peering down on them every half-aisle. In the food section Fanny noticed a strange package: "Synthomanna! What's it doing on the shelf, Leo? It's not supposed to be in circulation anymore. Who can we tell? There isn't a single clerk here."

Leo frowned. "Unless even Dr. Marc is out of the loop and this package is a new version that's supposedly safe. Do you think maybe there's been a reversal of the sterility effect?"

"I don't know. But even if it is safe, would you eat it? Would you take a chance?"

"Hell, no!" Leo retorted. "I wouldn't touch it. According to Marc, practically the entire planet got addicted to it before anyone even knew about the mutation consequence."

"So what's it doing here? Who can we tell? Should we say something to the camera that's recording everything? This is totally creepy, Leo."

"Yeah, it's weird all right. I suppose you could talk to the camera. Somebody must be monitoring them—maybe at the company that installed them. Of course they have no way of reaching us."

"I'll do it anyway," Fanny said. She tilted her head upward and spoke passionately in detail to the box above with its all-seeing Cyclops eye. Proud of herself, she wandered down the aisle and picked up several snack packets of cheese crackers wrapped in cellophane. "In case we get the hungries later."

Neither of them noticed a handful of other customers eyeing them with suspicion. The locals didn't often see shoppers freaking out in this place. More like never.

A block away they discovered the park. From their higher vantage point at street level, they were able to oversee the entire panorama in a mile-wide valley. A baseball diamond had been laid out at one end. Farther along, a thick stand of juniper, oak and cedar trees wrapped around a shimmering blue pond. A winding path led them through the trees and park benches right up to the pond's edge. A short rickety pier sat some fifty yards to their left. A sunken rowboat lay in the mud beside it, with a line securing it to a post as though it could actually float away.

"Oh, look, Leo, there's a loon diving straight into the water," an excited Fanny said, pointing to the middle of the pond. "It's the Minnesota state bird." The loon disappeared under ripples, then abruptly broke the surface with a small wriggling fish in its beak.

"I see a bunch of wood ducks over there in the reeds," Fanny said. "Let's go feed them."

"Feed them what?" asked Leo.

"These," she replied, pulling the cracker packs from her purse.

"I thought those were supposed to be for our lunch."

"Didn't your mother teach you to share? C'mon, let's go sit on the pier."

The pier was fragile and slightly cockeyed. Its dry, deep-grained wood reflected years-long neglect. At first they sat in the warm sun, cross-legged, but Fanny soon had her shoes and socks off and her backside positioned to dangle her legs over the side. She tested the water with the toes of her left foot first.

"Oooh! It's so cold," she yelled, pulling her foot out. After several more tries, she finally eased both feet in over her ankles. Leo followed suit.

*Damned cold,* he decided, but did his macho best to pretend that his ankles weren't getting numb. He surprised Fanny by putting an arm around her shoulders and pulling her close. She smiled and laid her head in the cleft of his shoulder. But only for a moment.

## Unto the Third Generation

By now the first of the wood ducks began venturing out of the reeds and swimming toward them to investigate the couple. Leo and Fanny watched the drake in speechless awe—his exquisite plumage of radiant blue, yellow, purple and russet. And his green head, red eyes and tri-colored beak. Tearing open the cellophane packets, Fanny broke the first cracker into pieces and tossed them within a yard of the drake. He snapped them up. Now alerted to a possible feeding frenzy, an armada of wood ducks left the safety of hollow tree trunks and tall, yellowed reeds and glided toward the pier. Fanny hastily threw more crackers bits into the water. She continued feeding the noisy *we-e-e-k-we-e-e-k-ing* ducks until her supply dwindled to none. Not in it for the conversation, the ducks soon retreated to the tree trunks and reeds, and their normal diet of insects, crustaceans, acorns and nuts.

It was mid-afternoon when Leo just couldn't sit any longer and tried to rise to his feet. With all of his weight concentrated on a single foot while leveraging himself up, a wood slat broke. He was barely able to maintain his balance and keep from falling into the water.

Fanny was not so lucky. The broken board caused her to shift sideways and forward. A lengthy sliver of wood pierced the inside of her left thigh. Screaming, she slipped into the pond, the water deep enough to cover her thighs. A quick-thinking Leo leaned down, grabbed her under her arms, and lifted her back onto the rickety pier. Fanny continued to scream with pain. He carried her in his muscular arms to the nearest park bench, where he laid her down to assess the damage.

Leo saw that a wood sliver, roughly a quarter-inch in diameter and about three inches long, had penetrated halfway up the inside of her left thigh. He couldn't know how deep. The wound was barely bleeding at the moment, but was awash in muddy water, stirred up from her feet hitting the pond bed. Leo thought, *There's a major artery in there somewhere. If I pull out the sliver now, she could bleed to death. I've got to get help. Marc will know what to do. I need a phone.* His taut stomach knotted up as he realized he had no phone of his own. Leo noticed Fanny's purse lying on the pier. Marc's iTalk would be in it. He left Fanny crying and ran back to retrieve the purse. Phone in hand, he found Marc's name at the top of the caller list. It rang only a few seconds when Marc answered.

"Marc, we've got an emergency here. We're in the park. Fanny has a monstrous wood sliver sticking out of her thigh and I'm afraid to remove it—she'll bleed to death. Can you come right away? We're at the last park bench closest to the duck pond."

"I'm on my way, Leo. Keep her calm and still. I'll be there in ten minutes." He hung up.

Leo returned and knelt before the bench, holding Fanny's head in his hands. Her screaming had been reduced to moans and sobs. Wondering whether she was in shock, he kissed her on the forehead, then told her Marc was on the way. She responded to the calming tone of his voice. At that moment he knew exactly what Fanny meant to him. *I'm totally committed to her. No question about it. I don't want to lose her.* Fanny drifted in and out of consciousness while they waited.

Out of the din of distant street sounds, a distinct whine grew louder and louder until Leo looked up and saw the Fleet Mayflower setting down in a wide spot on the lawn. The bubble hatch sprang up as Marc bounced to the ground and rushed to their side. One shot of antibiotics and another for her pain became the first order of business. Marc poured alcohol over the wound and cleaned around it.

"Good job, Leo. You were right not to remove the splinter. It appears to have punctured the femoral artery sheath. Luckily, it did not prevent blood flow to the lower leg altogether. My hospital is twenty miles away, too far, so we must get her back to the Kettle Farm in a hurry. I have everything I need there. Give me a hand and we'll stretch her out in the rear seat. Easy does it now."

The hovermobile rose up and sped all the way. This time Leo appreciated Marc's race driver mode. As they landed, Kitty Fairfield was waiting for them. Marc had called her on the way to the accident scene. Leo was relegated to his room while the two medics attended to Fanny in a sterile operating room on the first floor.

Leo stripped off his wet, muddy shorts and T-shirt, wishing now that they hadn't rushed the season. *If we'd been in jeans, her leg would've been protected. But enough with the guilt*, he decided, *I'm being stupid.* After showering and changing, he found the wall vision  annoying, and couldn't concentrate enough even to read the thriller he'd started. Jumping up, he walked the halls for half an hour, stopping to look out the windows at the placid lawns and trees with delicate new buds. *And the day was going so perfectly.* He returned to his room and paced back and forth until it seemed pointless. He dropped into the recliner and dozed off. Several hours later, he heard the sound of activity in Fanny's room. As he came through the door, Kitty and Marc were transferring her from a gurney to her bed. Fanny was sound asleep.

Composed and professional in her nurse's uniform, Kitty approached Leo with an outstretched hand. "Still friends?"

"Friends!" he repeated, taking her hand and shaking it. "Thank you for helping out today. I truly appreciate it."

"It's my job. I'm just glad I happened to be on duty," she said. Her voice softened. "Sorry about the way we ended our relationship, but I was in pretty bad shape at the time."

Leo nodded. "Oh, I understood. Finally." He hesitated, not sure how to put what he felt into words. "But I'm very sorry you didn't get what you wanted."

"Me too." Kitty spun about and hurried out of the room, pulling off her surgical over-garments as she left. Hurrying so no one could see her teary eyes, nor sense her inner regret. She had lost more than a baby.

Marc pulled the fresh covers over the patient and turned to confront a long-faced Leo. "Easy, man. Fanny will be fine, thanks to your smart thinking. She lost a little blood, but not enough to warrant a transfusion. I removed a tiny section of the femoral artery and stitched up the cut ends over a minimal shunt. Like any deep wound, it will take time and patience to heal. She'll be up and around in no time."

"Is there any chance of infection?" asked Leo. "Oh, God, is Fanny in any great pain now?"

"There's *always* a chance of infection. But I've cleaned the wound thoroughly and dosed her with antibiotics. I've also sedated her, so she'll probably sleep till morning. If she still has pain then, I can give her something for that as well."

"Afterward, will she have a limp?" he asked. "And will there be ugly scarring?"

"Any limp is highly unlikely since neither bone nor nerve is involved." Marc hesitated for a moment and then added, "As for scarring, I tried to minimize the invasiveness. My actual incision was less than two inches. A little time should cause the resulting scar to fade to almost unnoticeable."

Leo's towering frame and long arms embraced the small doctor in a bear hug. "Thanks, Marc," he said with an extra squeeze. "You don't know how grateful I am for saving my gal."

"Shucks, fella, t'weren't nuttin'," offered Marc in his best comic yokel imitation. "Wait! You said *my* gal. That suggests you two have already made up your mind to be a permanent item. Is it true? Are you sure?"

"Yeah, yeah!" replied Leo, releasing his grip on the doctor and stepping back a foot or two. "Only Fanny doesn't know yet. I only hope she hasn't changed *her* mind."

"Why would she change her mind?" asked Marc. "She was all in the last time I heard."

"Well, we had that argument at breakfast," replied Leo.

"I know. Has she said any more about it?" asked Marc.

"Yeah. Only *she* took it to mean we were incompatible. I meant no such thing."

Marc dismissed the conflict with a wave of his hand. "All things considered and what's at stake, I'm sure you two will come to an understanding. Go and relax now. She's most likely to be out of it until morning." He gave Leo a reassuring slap on the back and left the room, saying over his shoulder, "I've got some paperwork to do. It's not all fun and games in the OR."

Leo started to follow him, but changed his mind. In the corner by the window he spotted a padded side chair. After an initial shove, he slid it easily across the tiled floor next to the bed. He bent over and kissed Fanny's forehead—gently, as though it might wake her. He folded back the corner of her sheet. Taking her limp hand in his own, he lowered himself into the chair for the duration. There was no way she would wake up and not know he was there for her. He decided this was what love was all about.

Chapter 15

# Finding Fault
(The year 2085)

**T**WO GENERATIONS HAD PASSED SINCE THE PRIME number year 2039, and how remarkable it truly had been. Then, in 2079, the third generation had begun with the horrifying perception that there would be no new births, no new babies, and little hope for a mournful, ever-dying population. Scientists now knew the cause, but not the cure. Nearly everyone had taken advantage of the synthetic food Synthomanna, the wonder substance. Who could have resisted the facts, features and bravado put forth in the advertising—and, more important, the versatility and flavors in the food itself? Were any population segments spared? Those in charge had no knowledge of tribes and communities that lay hidden from society in the remotest reaches of the earth—nor of the existence of Fanny and Leo.

Statesmen looked to soothe their nations in the clutches of the catastrophe. Politicians sought to expose whoever was at fault. Scientists had another goal.

* * * *

**T**oday nearly a thousand delegates converged on The Hague, the Netherlands, to attend the Congress of Nations. The scientists' goal was to seek a course of reversing action—or to at least halt the calamitous spread of sterility. Delegates intended to investigate what went wrong in the universal adoption and acceptance of Synthomanna, and to determine whether any criminal action was warranted. The Executive Committee took most of a week to come up with an appropriate agenda. None of the original celebrants of the 2039 conference were in attendance, although each had been duly subpoenaed. Umberto Valeriani and Edvard Holgren had died. Vassally Krackob had been excused for mental health reasons; he had a nervous breakdown. Sarah Bet Moshez, the Israeli, hadn't responded; she was on sabbatical.

All the rituals and routine business were waived. The meat of the agenda was next. Chairman Pierre Montant, the former mayor of Lyon, France, manned the gavel.

"The chair recognizes the delegate from England: Lord Michael Morris, Earl of Shoeffield."

"Thank you," said Lord Morris, sporting a flamboyant mustache and forced grin. "While I sincerely admired Señoré Valeriani and all he hoped to accomplish, I do believe the crux of the matter goes back to the first nation to grant approval without sufficient testing. I challenge the delegate from Italy to produce the original test regimen and results for our scientific subcommittee to scrutinize."

The chair recognized the Italian delegate, Señoré Guillermo Faritzi, president of Faritzi Industries, where Italy's testing took place. In his thick English accent Faritzi spoke. "My illustrious colleague, Lord Morris, is quick to point, how you say, the finger. I assure you the test data and the rigors under which the tests were conducted will be provided with all due speed. But I ask you, honorable colleagues, how many years of further studies will be sufficient? Two years? Five? Ten? One hundred?"

"I thank the delegate for his cooperation," said Morris. "But I object to Señoré Faritzi's sarcasm. We are reasonable men here, tasked with a momentous course of action."

"I beg your pardon, Lord Morris," said Faritzi with controlled fury. "We studied for only sixteen years. We shared results with three other countries conducting parallel studies on the same end product."

Pierre Montant broke in. "Please name those countries now for this great assembly."

"Yes, of course!" responded Faritzi. "Sweden, Russia and Israel freely exchanged test results with us. Also, I believe the United States conducted some independent studies on Synthomanna."

Chairman Montant quickly interceded. "I propose that all known data on the product, regardless of country of origin, be forwarded to the select subcommittee as quickly as possible. All those in favor?" A sea of hands went up. "The ayes have it—unanimously, it appears!"

Dr. Edgar Grovann, president of Regus Centre Laboratories in Bordeaux, France, stood to be recognized. Chairman Montant nodded for him to proceed.

"I am most curious," Dr. Grovann began. "How much of this so-called testing was conducted on animals? At what point in the research were the first human trials conducted? I direct my question to Señoré Faritzi."

"During the fifth year of testing," was the quick response.

A murmur of skeptical voices rippled though the audience.

"Then can we assume that only eleven years of data have been collected on human use of the product?" asked Dr. Grovann.

No answer was forthcoming, except for louder murmurs from the audience, echoing the same conclusion.

Dr. Amos Roberts, a physician at Citizens General Hospital in Madison, Wisconsin, rose. "With all due respect to my honorable colleagues, I ask you this: How much of the research was directed toward individual taste, consistency, nourishment and booster components, and how much was directed toward the product's long-term effects?"

Faritzi jumped up to respond. "It's too difficult to say without collecting man-hours on the individual tasks. The select subcommittee might be able to break out those specific elements when they collect all the tests and results."

Dr. Roberts spoke again. Although in his sixties with a shock of white hair, he looked years younger. "I think from what all of us have heard here today, we can conclude that regardless of the amount of research done on the product, and the length of time devoted to studying side effects, it was not enough time by a long shot. We are a generation short of the real truth. Are we in agreement there?"

Audience chatter turned into a near-roar. The chair slammed his gavel down to restore order and obtained an aye vote by the assembly to write Dr. Roberts' conclusion into the record.

Dr. Bertrum Snyder, chairman of the U.S. Foods/Drugs/ Research Agency, spoke next, reading from a script he had thought-fully and diplomatically prepared. "I can sympathize with Señoré Faritzi's point of view. We at the FDRA face our own nightmares on this kind of question all the time. In reality, there is no pre-dictable measure of time to account for all the residual effects of widely differing unknown products. Most countries legislate what they believe is a reasonable amount of time to wait. The anomaly here is that this product took an unreasonable amount of time to rear its ugly head. To the best of my knowledge, no laws were bro-ken, yet all mankind will come to pay for our universally horrific mistake."

Dr. Snyder cleared his throat, drained an entire glass of wa-ter, then set his script down on the podium. He no longer needed to read. His impassioned words were etched into his brain. "Even if we agree on a specific number of years to legislate, it is no easy task, taking into account all the forces impacting on such a decision. We face two wildly opposing demands—monsters, actually—if we continue to produce Synthomanna as it is. There is the unspeak-able harm that will be perpetrated by causing sterility versus those millions whose lives are saved from famine. How many will die of hunger versus the decline and fall of the human race?

"On the opposite side, how much safety can we afford versus the sales revenue lost when we withdraw Synthomanna completely while we continue our research? This is not just a cynical business question. Hundreds of thousands of employees have already lost their jobs in factories where Synthomanna is no longer produced. Many companies out there are putting pressure on legislators from both sides."

Dr. Snyder's voice grew more commanding as he saw that he now owned the audience. "The enormous power of this great assembly must be turned away from searching for a scapegoat. Instead of placing blame and guilt, let us focus every ounce of our research on finding a way to reverse this evil result that has befallen us. Now, today, we scientists must return to our laboratories to resolve the two shortfalls in our past research. One: What element or compound in Synthomanna is causing sterility? And two: Can it be manufactured with other ingredients that are both harmless and still of nutritional value? I am confident that, with our combined expertise and commitment, we can come up with the answers."

He gazed out over a totally silent audience. After a few moments, a young scientist in the fifteenth row sprang up and began to vigorously applaud. Soon others rose in assent and joined him until the entire assembly became united in their new goal. Dr. Snyder had captured the essence of their hope.

Chapter 16

# A New World?

(The same year)

**H**OURS PASSED. AN OVERWHELMING DROWSINESS took hold of Leo. His slowly drooping forehead came to rest on the sheet next to Fanny's elbow. This is how Marc found them when he made his two nighttime checks on his patient. No need to disturb either one.

Dawn broke, sharing its stingy light through the drapes in the patient's room. Fanny's eyes fluttered open. She lay motionless for a time, collecting her senses. *I'm on my back. I never sleep on my back.* Instinctively, she shook her damp right hand, releasing it from somewhere. *Someone holding it?* Looking down, her eyes encountered a large head full of dark hair. *His!* She tried to pull away, to reposition her left leg out of its pillowed cradle. The slightest movement of that leg immediately sent a message of excruciating pain to her brain.

She screamed, so loud and penetrating that Leo awoke and jolted to an upright position. He tried to calm her. "Darling!" But a hysterical Fanny had thrown off her covers to see if her wounded limb was still there.

"My leg," she wailed. "It hurts!"

She writhed back and forth at a pain level Leo couldn't comprehend, so he scrambled for the call button. He found it tucked under her pillow and pressed it again and again. He tried to comfort her, cupping his hands around her cheeks. "I'm here, sweetheart. I'm here for you," he shouted. He thought she heard him and tried to take hold of her right hand, but she thrust it away.

"Leave me alone!" she cried. "Get away from me! Get out of here and leave me alone."

Her outcry left him helpless and devastated. He backed away from the bed and left the room.

In the hall he met Marc, rushing toward Fanny's room.

"Where are you going, Leo?"

"She needs you more than me," his sullen voice retorted. "Go to her, man."

Marc found her alternately sobbing and screaming, so he prepared a syringe with pain killer and administered it. In a few minutes, Fanny began to slowly calm down.

Marc pulled down the covers and placed her leg back into the cradle of pillows that had comforted her through the night.

"What happened in here?" he asked. "I just saw a much deflated Leo, rushing out of this room, saying that you needed me more than him. What did he mean by that? Did you fight?"

"I don't know," replied Fanny, still disoriented. "I was in pain, scared, and out of my head mostly. I don't remember saying anything specific."

Marc handed her a pill. "Take this now. It's a sedative." Marc took her temperature, listened to her heart, and checked her pulse. Satisfied, he unwrapped her wound, cleaned around it, painted it with a new coat of antiseptic gel, and re-bandaged the leg. He left her with the promise that he would look in on her later in the day.

* * * *

**F**anny slept, read for a while, and slept a good deal more. A delivery boy dropped off her lunch, a tuna sandwich and carton of milk. Shortly after six that evening Marc reappeared with her dinner tray. He sat while she ate the microwaved chicken pot pie.

"Where's Leo?" she asked between bites. "He hasn't been

in to see me all day. Is he all right?"

"I don't know," Marc said, shrugging his shoulders and turning his palms up. "He wasn't in his room, and all his things are gone. I think he's left us for good, Fanny."

"Gone! How? Why?"

"I think *you* had better rethink what you said to the man this morning."

"I haven't the faintest idea what I said. I was out of my head with pain. I don't remember anything other than being extremely angry. I don't even know why. Do you really think I took my anger out on Leo?"

"Yes." Marc put his hand atop hers, trying to be sympathetic.

"Where would the poor guy go?"

Marc shook his head. "I was at breakfast with you yesterday. The two of you had a heated discussion when he mentioned he preferred to live someplace warm."

Fanny's eyes widened, frantic and fearful. "Oh, Marc, no. Did he at least leave a note?"

"Not exactly."

"What do you mean—not exactly?"

"Leo did leave us a sterile container filled with his semen in the freezer. I saw it when I got the pot pie out for your dinner. He labeled it so I wouldn't throw it out."

"But I was hoping for so much more than that. We both wanted intimacy. I looked forward to love and marriage. I thought he wanted that, too. Her eyes turned smoky and her lips pouted. "How callous of him to reject me, to leave without saying goodbye. How could I have been so wrong?"

The doctor took a moment to frame his words. He'd witnessed that scene at breakfast when Fanny behaved like a bratty, spoiled child. "I'm guessing Leo felt that *you* were rejecting *him*. And from the hall, just this morning, I heard you yell at him to get out and leave you alone. I believe he did want love, my dear. Otherwise, why would he have taken such good care of you yesterday?

He spent the whole night at your bedside, holding your hand."

Fanny's ample body fell into a dejected slump. Marc's words rang true. A realization of loss set in, triggering a fit of sobbing. "It's all my fault," she whispered.

Marc handed her the box of tissues and left the room. A few minutes later, he returned with a collapsible aluminum walker. He set it in position next to the bed and threw back the covers.

"Okay, young lady, we're going to get you up and walking."

"So soon?" she whimpered.

"Yep! Can't having you drown in a sea of your own tears, or have your muscles atrophy. Besides, you have some important business to attend to."

"Business?" she whined. "What kind of business?" She dabbed at her eyes with a fresh tissue.

"One, are you just letting him go without inquiring after him? And two, are you throwing away the insemination opportunity he left behind? I can administer it, you know."

Marc gently lifted her leg out of its cradle and assisted her in turning so that both legs hung over the edge of the bed. She cringed in anticipation of pain, reaching for the walker as she slid her bottom off the side of the bed and both feet onto the floor. Surprised that it didn't hurt as much as she thought it would, she took two careful steps and reset the walker a short distance in front of her.

"How long will I have to use this contraption?" she asked, taking two more steps.

"Until you feel safe and comfortable without it. I can get you a cane, if you prefer."

"No!" Her self-pity was soon replaced by the distraction of walking again. Twice across the room and she abandoned the walker. Next, she traveled into the corridor and ambitiously headed for one end of it. Tiring on the return trip, she headed to her recliner. She caught her breath, then picked up the anchor-speak on the end table.

"Taxi dispatcher in Pucevale," she asked the operator...

"Hello. Can you tell me the drop-off point for the fare you picked up at the Pucevale Kettle Farm this morning, say between ten and noon?....Why?....Uh, because he left something valuable behind. I need to reach him.  It's very important....I should try the hover-bus station? Oh, dear. Thank you."

She looked up at Marc. "He's probably on an aerobus well on its way to Minneapolis by now."

"You can always try the airlines," said Marc. "They have flight manifests they can check. I'll leave you to your detective work. I've got some work to do."

* * * *

The deadline for facility shutdown was only two days off. Fanny's leg was on the mend, free and clear of infection, and she was getting around with little or no difficulty. She had access to the entire facility, as Marc had unlocked all of the previously forbidden doors. But there was no fun in exploring. Her last resort, calls to the airlines, had proven mostly uncooperative. One did promise to deliver a call-home message if his name turned up on any of their flight manifests. Fanny's guilt weighed heavily on her, even though there were fewer tears now.

After the last bandage came off, Marc still stopped off at her room for a short chat a few times each day between his many closing-out chores. She was sitting and reading when he came in.

"Fanny, it's Wednesday already and we have to be out of here by noon on Friday. They're coming to board the place up. I've got a truck scheduled this afternoon to pick up all the useful fixtures, instruments and supplies. Have you decided where you're relocating yet?"

She gave a deep sigh. "I want to stay here as long as possible in case the airline calls. I talked with a lady who runs a rooming house in Minneapolis. She's holding a room for me, starting tomorrow night. I'll have to take the afternoon aerobus the next day as a last resort, but I won't stop looking for Leo."

"I completely understand." Marc held up his hand, palm out. "My iTalk is vibrating." He pulled it out of his breast pocket and answered. "Leo! Where the hell are you? You're still in Puce-vale?...Fanny's fine. She's here in the room with me and she desperately wants to speak to you....No, I tell you, she's fine....No, damn it, don't hang up. Here she is." He held out the phone to an agitated Fanny, whose shaking hand almost dropped it.

"Leo! Sweetheart! I love you and want to spend the rest of my life with you. I apologize for the way I treated you. I was clear out of my head with pain. Please forgive me. I've been so worried that I wouldn't find you. I've been trying ever since you left. Come back here this afternoon and we'll decide together where we'll go from here....No, I'll go anywhere you want, even move to a warmer climate, only come back here for me. I love you. I can't wait to see and hold you." She handed the phone back to Marc.

"Well?"

"He's coming back." Her face lit up with joy and relief.

* * * *

**F**anny took the elevator down to the lobby and waited. And waited. Half an hour later, she heard the hovercab engine outside the building. Trying not to overwork her healed leg, she half-trotted to the front door and burst outside.

The bubble hatch was already up, and Leo sprang to the ground. Fanny couldn't wait. She ran straight at him and jumped into his arms. The vehicle rose and sped away, leaving the two in a tight embrace. They smothered each other with kisses. Finally, they walked hand in hand back into the building, up the elevator, and straight into her room. When they got to her door, he picked her up, carried her across the threshold, and set her down on the edge of the bed. He returned to close the door and lock it.

"Fanny, I will marry you," he said. "We can wait to make love if you like."

"Hell, no!" she mumbled and pulled him close.

She unbuttoned his shirt and slid her hands inside to feel the smooth touch of his massive chest. She buried her face there while he slipped out of the shirt altogether and worked on the two pearl buttons at the nape of her neck. She helped him pull her blouse over her head. Next she attacked his belt and made short shrift of pulling off his pants. Amid the flurry of undressing, they whispered many words of affection and praises and promises. And when the last stitch of clothing had been cast aside, they stood face to face for a solitary minute, soaking up all that they had imagined and dreamt of. Leo lifted his Fanny once more and laid her down in the center of her bed. He climbed in after her. They caressed and moaned in a slow, sensual, and finally urgent manner until their private world erupted into pure pleasure. They lay there for some time, then re-created a second flight to sheer paradise. It was after that and only then that they began to speak of their future.

* * * *

Friday morning relentlessly arrived. The remaining three residents gathered in the lobby, packed and ready to leave for good. It was goodbye time.

"Sit down," ordered Marc, after uncharacteristically pacing back and forth for ten minutes. "I shouldn't let you two go without some sort of pep talk. I can't claim to be much of a philosopher, but as I'm the only one left here, I guess that makes me the resident seer. I feel I have a responsibility to warn you."

Seated on the vinyl couch, Fanny and Leo looked at one another with the word "warn" on their minds. They were prepared to pay attention.

"Listen," said Marc. "You're going out into a world drastically changed by innovation, but still manipulated by age-old motives. Here in the United States democracy prevails, but runs a delicate and hazardous path through a jungle of power, wealth and greed. War, fear and cruelty remain alive in countries still under despotism. Famine will return. Not much can be done about that right now. As you know, an honorable effort to defeat famine turned into a debacle. But the good news is, scientists are now working on a new, safe synthetic food. And, thank God, a scattering of individuals around the world chose not to partake of Synthomanna—or, living in remote corners, never even knew about it. Those blessed individuals are not sterile."

Marc paused to acknowledge the couple's intent looks and clasped hands. They were paying serious attention. "Those living in their third generation will come to the end of their lives in another forty to sixty years. Find help and glean wisdom from them while they live. It will be your responsibility to pass along to your children all the good lessons you've learned. Hey, I know I'm laying a heavy load on you, but I also know you're both up to the job. The two of you, and other survivors like you, will be the Adams and Eves of a new world."

With tears in her eyes, Fanny set her luggage on the floor and hugged Marc for the last time. Leo followed with his big-arm embrace and a healthy slap on Marc's back. Marc pulled back the door to reveal a silver hovercab outside. He watched as the cabbie stowed their luggage and closed the hatch over the top of his passengers. A hum morphed into a higher pitch as the anti-gravitational machine rose above the pavement, turned toward the road between the double row of cedars, and shot forward.

Marc watched the silver machine grow smaller and darker as it sped away, a mere dot, then a memory. *It will be up to those two, and other brave souls like them, to fulfill the promise of the world to come.*

### THE END

**Rosemary and Larry Mild**, cheerful partners in crime, coauthor mysteries and thrillers. Their short stories appear in three anthologies: *Dark Paradise:* Mysteries in the Land of Aloha; *Mystery in Paradise:* 13 Tales of Suspense; and Chesapeake Crimes: *Homicidal Holidays.* In 2013 the Milds waved goodbye to Severna Park, Maryland, and moved to Honolulu, Hawaii, where they cherish time with their children and grandchildren. The Milds are members of Mystery Writers of America, Sisters in Crime and Hawaii Fiction Writers.

Visit them at **www.magicile.com**.
Contact them at **roselarry@magicile.com**.

# Also by Rosemary and Larry

### The Paco and Molly Mystery Series

***Locks and Cream Cheese***—In scandal-ridden Black Rain Corners, a Chesapeake Bay mansion harbors locked rooms and deadly secrets. A wily detective and a gourmet cook tackle the case.

***Hot Grudge Sunday***—Bank robbers and conspirators derail the sleuths' blissful honeymoon at the Grand Canyon. Can they nail the suspects after they themselves become targets?

***Boston Scream Pie***—A teenage girl's nightmare triggers a sinister tale of twins, two warring families, and a blonde bombshell who hates being called "Mom."

**Available on Amazon.com
and as E-Books**

# Also by Rosemary and Larry

## The Dan and Rivka Sherman Mystery Series

***Death Steals A Holy Book***—Dan and Rivka inherit a rare Yiddish translation of a 14th-century holy book, but it is stolen and their book restorer is murdered. Can they recover the book and nail the culprit?

***Death Goes Postal***—Priceless 15th-century typesetting artifacts journey through time, leaving a sinister imprint in their wake. Dan and Rivka risk life and limb to recover the treasures. Not quite what they expected when they bought The Olde Victorian Bookstore.

***Death Takes A Mistress***—After 23 years, Ivy Cohen seeks revenge on the lover who killed her mother. She follows the clues from London to Maryland, where she makes a shocking discovery.

**Available on Amazon.com
and as E-Books**

# Also by Rosemary and Larry

***Murder, Fantasy, and Weird Tales*—**
Delve into tales of the brave, the fool-
hardy, and the wicked on their journeys to
the unknown in Hawaii, Japan, Cambodia,
Italy, and elsewhere. Art lovers, hit women,
a vampire, a lively hologram, and others
reveal their secret compulsions.

***Cry Ohana, Adventure and Suspense
in Hawaii*—**A car accident and murder
tear apart a Hawaiian *ohana* (family). Danger erupts at a Filipino wedding, a Maui
resort, and amid the Big Island's volcanic
steam vents. Can the family re-unite and
bring down the killer?

***The Misadventures of Slim O. Wittz,
Soft-Boiled Detective*—**If you're looking
for a truly bumbling gumshoe, you want
me, Slim. I'm rarely in charge, frequently
behind the eight ball and seldom paid;
but in spite of all that, my case record is
remarkably shaky.

**Available on Amazon.com
and as E-Books**

# Also by Rosemary

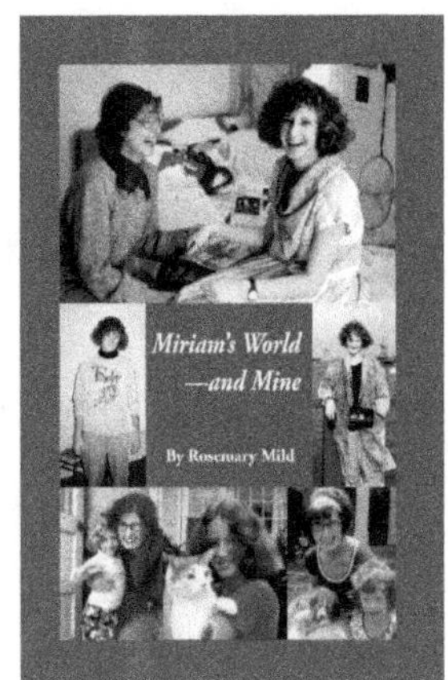

***Miriam's World—and Mine***
Miriam Luby Wolfe, a junior at Syracuse U., spent her fall semester in London exploring her talents: singing, dancing, acting, and writing. But she never made it home. A terrorist bomb destroyed her plane over Lockerbie, Scotland. Learn about Miriam, the Pan Am families, the bombers, and the political fallout.

***Love! Laugh! Panic! Life with My Mother***—Rosemary's hilarious and heartwarming story of her super-achieving mother. Luby Pollack was a journalist, popular book author, and psychiatrist's wife. Always the Heroine, and sometimes the Villain, from the viewpoint of her loving but ornery daughter.

**Available on Amazon.com
and as E-Books**